ABSOLUTION

CATHARSIS BOOK ONE

TEFFETELLER MYART

Book Cover by Quirky Circe Book Design

Proofreader: Roxana Coumans

CONTENTS

— • —

PROLOGUE

"I could never deny you anything, babygirl."

Gloria flinched. She *hated* when he called her that, like no time had passed since they'd been together, like he'd not burned that bridge like it was a savage vampire he needed to destroy.

She had spent two years trying her hardest to recover from what he had done to her. Through every action she took, the books she wrote, the men she dated, she had been trying—for *two years*—to move past him.

And there she was. Back in his country, back in his house, about to ruin her life all over again. She knew he hadn't changed; he was exactly the same man who had come into Gloria's life two years earlier and turned it upside down. She'd left Georgia—and her family's protection—to go be with this vile, cruel man across the Atlantic. She'd moved to England to be with him. She'd turned her back on said family, and on their fortune, to which she had been an heiress, before *she* had burned *that* bridge...and she'd done it all for him.

For that fucking man.

"You're a liar, Henry," Gloria said, lifting her head and squaring her shoulders as she stared at him. "You lie to everyone. To all the women you sleep with, to your family...but most of all, you lie to yourself. You truly believe that you're a gentleman, don't you?"

"I've not knocked you flat yet. You still believe yourself to be the victim, I see."

"Henry."

"If you didn't want to be here, you wouldn't have come here. You wanted everything that I did with you back then, and you want it again, now. Why else would you be standing in my living room again, Gloria Alexander?"

1

— ◆ —

CHAPTER ONE

Gloria had learned a lot in the two years since she'd become a submissive.

She'd started out as almost completely innocent. She'd been a sheltered, thirty-year-old woman living on her family's estate in Atlanta. She had dated a few men in her teenage years, but one bad experience when she was twenty had turned her against dating for years...until her family had arranged for her to meet who they considered to be a "nice man;" he'd been a clueless forty-year-old, with no sexual experience, who had left Gloria with zero satisfaction, making her think of the act of sex with dread, as she'd become accustomed to no passion (and no pleasure, for that matter), due to her boyfriend's selfish, clumsy lack of experience...and lack of willingness to try.

It had apparently felt good to *him,* and that had been all that mattered.

It was no wonder, then, that Gloria had fallen so hard for the first man who came along to awaken her sexuality, to show her what sex was about...to guide her into giving into her instinctual desires, not those that society had engrained into her practically from birth.

Then he'd turned on her, emotionally tortured her...and it was no wonder that she'd become a needy, emotionally-starved woman desperate to submit to anyone who pretended to give half a shit about her.

That was in her past, though.

Sometimes Gloria couldn't help but to think back on the way she'd once been...particularly on days such as that one, when she had a book signing scheduled. Seeing the physical manifestations of all of her work for the past three years, from concept to publication, to her rise to fame as an author, was an emotional experience for her. She tended toward nostalgia at the best of times, so it all made sense.

It made sense to Gloria that she was thinking about Henry that day, that morning as she sat at her bathroom counter putting on her makeup, getting ready to go down to fucking

Barnes & Noble for a book signing; she'd graduated past signings at local libraries and smaller bookstores—not that those hadn't been wonderful opportunities—to having a huge banner outside Barnes & Noble, announcing the date of her book signing a couple of weeks in advance. She'd come so far, she was actually moderately wealthy by the standards of most people...being, she could afford her own home without roommates, could pay off her bills each month, could eat fresh produce, and had a car that wasn't twenty years old. She wasn't anywhere near as wealthy as she'd been before she'd turned her back on her family, but she wasn't broke anymore, and she had her *own* money, that *she* had earned.

She had all she'd ever wanted, so it made perfect sense that, as she lined her lower lip with lipliner, she was thinking about Henry.

About how, despite the time that had passed and everything else that had happened in her life, Gloria still felt like she'd lost out on something vital, something that made her, *her*...when she'd left Henry, she'd left a part of herself behind along with him, and no matter how successful she became and how many men she dated, she would never find that same sense of self that she'd had in Henry's arms.

Gloria applied her lipstick, then she stood, smoothing her dress, checking herself over in her mirror...she was ready to go. She wasn't naive enough to believe that her ability to write entertaining books was all that mattered when it came to being an author; as an erotica writer, there were certain expectations for her appearance. She had to look perfect, she had to be sexy and professional at the same time. She'd used some of her money for botox, which she got done every few months, and she'd hired a personal trainer and she worked out every day. She shopped a lot, and she got her nails and hair done, she received spa treatments regularly. Maintaining her physical appearance was paramount to her success in life.

She'd learned that.

She left her en suite bathroom and went to her bedroom, going into her walk-in closet to choose her handbag and shoes for the day. She should have done so the night before, when she'd chosen her outfit, but she also had to choose her accessories...all things that should not have been left until the last minute.

Gloria had been exhausted the night before, though, and she'd wanted to get to bed a little earlier, since she was getting up early to work out and get ready for the book signing...*and* she'd made a lot of progress on her new book that evening, and she hadn't wanted to tear herself away from it in order to accessorize her outfit...although she was paying the price for it that morning.

She quickly chose her go-to oversize leather tote bag, and some yellow leather sandals that matched the bag and went well with her black with dark-grey pinstripe jumpsuit she was wearing to the signing.

She went to her jewelry holder on the island in her closet and chose a chunky gold necklace. As she fastened the chain around her neck, Gloria saw the collar she had hanging up behind a large stack of her other gold jewelry, and she cringed...that was almost enough, right there, to make her want to call in and cancel the signing, to end up locked in her bedroom all day, thinking about all she'd lost, despite all she had gained.

She still hurt. Every relationship that ended made her hurt...and it was why she wrote.

She put on her black obsidian bead bracelet, then her rose quartz on top of it, and her watch on her right wrist, along with a gold bracelet. She added a gold ring with a jade stone to her right ring finger...and her left ring finger was still conspicuously bare. She was still getting used to it...

But her black heart tattoo was still there. It was faded and she'd not bothered to get it touched up, any of the times she'd been to the tattoo shop...her tattoo artist had offered every time she'd been in, but she'd refused. She was stubborn, not wanting to cover Henry's heart with anything else...but also not wanting to admit defeat by getting her heart touched up... Gloria feared getting it touched up would mean that Henry still held power over her...which was true, but not something her Sagittarius Venus wanted to admit to.

The ring she'd worn for eight months was gone, along with her marriage. *That* was the thing, that particular morning, that made Gloria want to dissolve on the floor in tears. *She* hadn't been the one to walk away from that marriage...although her ex-husband blamed her for their marriage falling apart.

Gloria knew that if she allowed herself to think about things too much, she would break down completely, so instead, she swallowed and left the bedroom, down the hall-way, past the guest room/office—where she did the majority of her writing—and to her open-concept living room/dining room/kitchen.

She grabbed a smoothie her trainer had suggested that she drink each morning, to take with her to the bookstore, then she locked up and headed for the elevator to the garage underneath her complex.

Gloria had bought her car before she'd gotten married. She was lucky that her husband had been wealthy of his own accord, or she could have lost a lot...as it was, he had more money than her, and he'd agreed to the settlement, of them keeping what they'd started with when they'd been married...and they were married such a short amount of time that they'd not had time to get a lot of assets together to have to split, but he'd gotten part of her eighteen-month royalties...and she'd gotten part of his income as a financial advisor.

Her husband had lived in a studio apartment. She'd been completely happy there in that small space with him, when she'd moved in with him—after they'd been dating for six months—but after their divorce was final, she'd used part of his money, along with hers, to rent a two-bedroom apartment in North Hollywood. She enjoyed the extra space...or, she told herself that she did, to make up for her loneliness.

She'd dated her ex-husband for six months before she left the Hollywood district apartment she'd shared with a roommate for nearly a year, where she'd lived when she first moved to Los Angeles, to move in with him. After living together for six months, they'd gotten married. They hadn't had a ceremony, they'd simply gone to the courthouse, then had gone out for dinner and drinks with Cynthia and Jordan—Gloria's roommate and her boyfriend, who had moved into Gloria's apartment with Cynthia when Gloria had moved in with her ex. She hadn't wanted a big wedding...probably due to the fact that she had been engaged to Henry, and their marriage had fallen through—albeit Gloria had been the one to walk away, in that case—so she hadn't wanted to take the time to plan out an elaborate wedding (not that she'd had anyone to invite to it), so they had eloped.

She missed her husband, every single day.

Gloria unlocked the door to her black Ford Taurus and got in, checking her phone one last time before she headed for Barnes & Noble. Her assistant—Cynthia, also her former roommate and best friend—was meeting her there, so she was just checking to make sure that there had been no last-minute changes in plan.

She had no new messages from Cynthia, so she headed on to the bookstore as planned, sipping her smoothie as she navigated the god-awful L.A. traffic.

Gloria hadn't had a terrible time adjusting to the traffic when she'd moved to Los Angeles, being from Atlanta. Traveling around her hometown had been challenging enough, when she'd ventured from her family's rural estate to the city, when she'd been earning her bachelor's degree in creative writing from Emory University. She'd grown accustomed to the traffic there, driving through the heart of the city to get from her family's estate to her college, and back.

Despite that fact, she still didn't enjoy driving in Los Angeles, and she thought that people who *did* enjoy it were most likely either masochists—not that she wouldn't have known anything about that—or had some sort of Stockholm syndrome with the city itself, putting their love for living there over their mental health.

She was as guilty as anyone else.

Finally she made it to the parking lot across from the shopping center where the bookstore was located, none too soon since she'd finished her smoothie and she desperately needed the restroom before she spent hours happily signing books for her much-loved readers.

She'd barely gotten her car locked before she turned around and Cynthia was there, dressed immaculately, her curly brown hair piled atop her head. She looked stressed, but she smiled, being as positive as possible. Cynthia was Gloria's closest friend, and had been for years. She knew her better than anyone, and she knew that Gloria had been absolutely gutted by her divorce, and how she struggled every day.

"Are you doing alright today?"

"I just have to pee."

Cynthia nodded. "Come with me."

"How are you?" Gloria asked, as they walked toward the back entrance of the building.

"You mean since we spoke two hours ago? I'm fine, Gloria."

"Thank you for coming early, and..."

Cynthia nodded, holding the door open for her. "I can't guarantee that none of your fans will ask any questions, but I've already spoken to everyone else here helping with today, and they all know what they can and cannot ask you."

"Good." Gloria sighed.

Cynthia gripped her friend's shoulder. "Are you sure you're up to this?"

Gloria shook her head. "I'm not up to it, but I'm doing it, anyway."

"I'm proud of you."

Because Cynthia knew what a challenge it was for Gloria, and how far she'd come from locking herself in her bedroom for days at a time when she'd first moved to L.A.

She'd been there to witness it.

Gloria would have instantly admitted that it wasn't her finest hour, but she hadn't believed that she would survive Henry, so she supposed that everything she had accomplished and what she'd made of herself in the two years since she'd last seen him—since she'd left him—was something to take pride in.

She'd thought of Henry that morning, sure, but the reason she was devastated was due to the fact that she was still in mourning over her marriage ending. Henry was so far in her past that he was little more than an errant thought from time to time.

Gloria could try convincing herself of *that* all she wanted, but deep-down she knew the truth of why she couldn't break that goddamned connection she seemed to have with her ex.

They'd shared too much.

She had been engaged to Henry, but she'd been *married* to her ex-husband,

But Bryson had promised her a family...and she had promised Henry the same.

And they'd both been let down, her and Henry both...and no matter what, Gloria knew that the reason she and Henry hadn't worked out had been due to her lack of ability to give him a baby...that was when things had started falling apart.

"Gloria," Cynthia said, concern evident in her voice, when she got a look at Gloria's face when she exited the restroom stall.

"What?" Gloria asked—as casually as possible—as she stepped up to wash her hands.

Cynthia grabbed her shoulder and stood behind her, studying her face in the mirror. "I know you're about to freak out."

Gloria let out a shaky breath. "Today is rough."

Cynthia sighed. "Fuck, I knew that you weren't ready for this. I can cancel—"

"Absolutely *not*," Gloria said. "I won't let my fans down."

"Don't you think your mental health is a little more important?"

"Than my career?" Gloria shook her head. "You've been the only person to be with me through all of this. You know me better than anyone. You know how much this means to me, and how much I love my readers."

"Your readers love you and wouldn't want you to be hurting while you're meeting them," Cynthia countered.

"Do you really believe that?"

"Yes. Even if they don't, *I* love you. I won't let you push yourself too far. It's part of my job, and you pay me well for it."

"I know. But I promise you that I'm fine." Gloria dug her lipgloss out of her handbag and applied it. "It would hurt worse to let Bryson ruin this day for me."

"Okay, Gloria." Cynthia frowned. "But I am keeping my eye on you. If you start freaking out, we leave. Do you understand me?"

"Yes," she agreed.

Cynthia frowned. "Good. Okay, let's go."

The first part of Gloria's book signing went perfectly. She was introduced and briefly interviewed by an employee, and—as promised—Cynthia had made sure that Gloria wasn't asked any intrusive questions, and nothing at *all* about her personal life or her divorce.

Then she began signing books and meeting her fans, taking photos with them. She was having a wonderful time, humbled—as always—that so many people were willing to give her a chance, to trust her to entertain them with her books that they spent their money on.

Thankfully it happened toward the end of the signing...or, when it was scheduled to end, although Gloria planned to stay as long as Barnes & Noble would allow, until she'd signed each book and taken as many photos as she was asked to...when one person asked a question, out of genuine concern for her, Gloria knew, although terribly intrusive and misguided.

She was a woman probably in her mid-forties, who had a well-worn copy of Gloria's debut novel for her to sign.

Gloria was writing the woman a note, when she asked, "What happened to you and Bryson?"

Gloria nearly dropped the pen, which would have ruined the woman's book. She swallowed hard, starting to sweat as she stammered and tried to finish writing a somewhat coherent note, while inside she was flipping out.

"Um...well...we just didn't work out."

She tried to give the woman a dismissive smile as she slid the book back across the table, but she felt her lips tremble.

Cynthia stepped in, grabbing Gloria's arm. "Sorry, everyone. Book signing is over. We've got to go."

"Cynthia, I—"

"Don't argue with me," she said, pulling Gloria out of her seat and pulling her across the room to the back of the store, where they'd entered, hours earlier.

"Cynthia, I need to go back there. There were still people in line, and—"

"And you're crying," Cynthia said, grabbing some tissues out of nowhere before Gloria had the chance to wipe away her tears with her fingers. "I can't believe she asked you that. Wonder how she would have liked it if you'd asked how many times *she's* been divorced?"

"I don't think she meant to upset me—"

"Doesn't matter," Cynthia insisted. "She did something stupid, so I cut the signing short...although you went half an hour over. You don't owe people access to you, especially not when they violate boundaries like that." She frowned. "But you wouldn't believe that, would you? Who am I kidding?"

"Cynthia..."

"I'm sorry, Gloria," Cynthia said, her voice softer. "I'm clearly not upset with you. I just can't get over the audacity of people."

"I'm okay," Gloria said. "It caught me off-guard. Maybe I can still go back out there, and—"

"Absolutely not," Cynthia said. "You go home and get some rest. You've had enough for today."

"Enough of what, though?" Gloria asked, slightly amused. "All I did was a book signing."

"Are you listening to yourself? That's huge."

Gloria smiled. "I know, I guess you're right. And I appreciate you looking out for me, always. I don't say that enough."

"Gloria, don't take this the wrong way, but you need someone to tell you when you take on too much. You're terrible at managing yourself."

"I know I am."

"Go home and rest. Take care of yourself. Do you want to have brunch tomorrow around eleven?"

"Yes. Then do you want to come back to my apartment and hang out?"

Cynthia nodded. "We need to catch up. I feel like we've not done that in a while...we talk about work all the time, but never anything fun."

"Well...you were there for me months ago, and that was a lot."

"I'll always be there for you, Gloria."

"Thank you."

Cynthia hesitated a moment, then she pulled Gloria in for a hug. "Always. You're the best friend I ever had."

"Me too," Gloria replied.

And it was true. Cynthia had been pretty much Gloria's whole family after she'd settled in L.A., as she'd left her home and family and the man she'd given up everything for. She'd had nothing and Cynthia had made her feel like she was loved and that she wasn't alone.

Gloria pulled away. "Thank you."

"Call me tonight. I'll see you in the morning."

"Okay."

Gloria felt deflated as she made her way across the parking lot to her Taurus. She always felt that way after she finished a book, or after an event, because of all the buildup and work and gratification, then it was over, and she forgot who she was for a while, until she moved onto a new project or attended a new event...but it was amplified that time.

When she'd finished her latest book, Gloria had still been married to Bryson. He'd taken her out that night for dinner at a nice restaurant, they'd come home to his studio apartment they shared, then...

Well, it had been a wonderful night.

And if he hadn't divorced her, then he would have come to her signing with her, and they would have gone home together afterward and it would have been another wonderful night; as it stood, Gloria was planning to go home and to lock herself in her bedroom until she could pull herself back together.

Because when she was in a mood like that one, there was nothing else that she *could* do.

Gloria unlocked her car and tossed her handbag in the passenger seat. She was about to sit down, when someone called to her.

"Gloria."

She froze, her hand on the top of her car. She started shaking, recognizing the voice immediately.

She would have recognized it anywhere, having heard it every day for eighteen months.

She took a deep breath. "Bryson."

2

— • —

Chapter Two

Gloria looked up to see her ex-husband striding across the parking lot toward her car. She shuddered, wishing that she hadn't stopped to see who'd been speaking to her, that she'd just closed her door and driven home.

She wasn't strong enough to *deal* with Bryson that particular day, although he *had* been on her mind the whole day, through everything she'd done.

He stopped by her car, holding onto the door, like he was afraid she'd slam it and drive away without talking to him.

"What do you need, Bryson?" she asked, staring at the ground as she spoke to him.

"I saw you had a signing here today. I mean, how could I have missed it? But, I'm happy for you, Gloria. You've come a long way."

She stared at him.

Bryson cleared his throat. "How are you doing?"

She laughed. "Really?"

"Please," he said.

She shook her head. "I don't have the emotional capacity to deal with you today. I don't know why you even came here."

"I wanted to come in and see you during your signing, but I thought that Cynthia might have me arrested."

"She probably would have."

He laughed. "Gloria, can't we be cordial to each other?"

She flinched. "I wanted to stay *married* to you."

"So you say."

She felt an intense burning anger deep in her stomach. His fucking *audacity* really got to her, cut her deeply...that another man she loved so intently had not only ended their relationship, but was also *taunting* her over it, refusing to allow her to move on...

Just like Henry had done, still following her on social media, following that last text message she'd sent to him on the plane from Vancouver, Washington back to L.A., after things hadn't worked out with her *new* dominant, the one who had been meant to replace Henry.

Gloria had never chased men before Henry...only him.

She had been so hurt over Donovan that she'd immediately text Henry on the plane back. She had been stupid, thinking that maybe he'd had time to think about what had happened and their relationship, and that he might even apologize, that they could repair what was left of what they'd once had.

How are you? she had asked him, seeing that he was online.

...

She'd grown to hate the goddamn ellipses she had seen so many times in the past, waiting for him to type out a text to her while they'd been dating online, before they'd met. They'd had so many fights before they'd even met, and he'd broken her heart more times than she could count.

And she'd been hurt and desperate enough to give him the opportunity to do it again, when she'd text him.

I'm fine, Henry had finally replied. Is there something that you want? I don't enjoy small talk.

She still remembered that pain, of not only finally having to accept that her relationship with Henry was truly over, but also that, after all he'd done to her, he could still be cruel.

She'd given up on him, after one last short conversation that had left her more broken than she had been before, hurting over Donovan.

Instead, she'd returned to Los Angeles grieving the loss of two relationships...

So, sitting there in her car with her ex-husband berating her didn't sit well with Gloria at all...especially since all that she wanted to do was to curl up in his arms and to beg him to get back together with her, even after everything.

"So I say?" she demanded. "No. I loved you with everything that I had in me. I...god, I still do."

He frowned.

She looked down. "I know. I shouldn't have said that."

"You've always been painfully honest about your feelings."

She nodded. Then, after only a moment's hesitation, she met his eyes again. "I never wanted to get a divorce. I still don't understand why *you* did. What did I do to you to make you stop loving me?"

"Can I just take you for a coffee or something? We should talk."

"Why?"

"Because I need to make sure you're doing okay."

"I'll save you five dollars on a fucking coffee and I'll tell you right now that I'm not okay. Not at all."

He flinched, like the idea of her being in pain physically hurt him. It was such bullshit, the same shit Henry and Donovan had pulled...the same shit her ex-boyfriend—the one *before* Bryson—had pulled. Fake empathy that was really only guilt at seeing that their power over a woman had disastrous results when he got tired of giving her the affection and security she needed.

"I want to leave."

"Please. At least tell me what you're up to."

"Writing books," she said. "No shit."

"Please."

She knew it was toxic of her to do it. She was only going to hurt herself.

But maybe once he spent some time with her, he'd realize what a mistake he'd made. Of course Gloria had signed the papers, once he'd refused counseling. She'd known he would only grow to resent her, otherwise.

So she allowed him to end their marriage.

She finally nodded. "Fine."

"Okay. Well..."

She checked her watch. "May as well make it drinks, Bryson. It's six o'clock. If I drink coffee now I'll never sleep tonight."

"Um...well, I guess."

She sat back in her seat, crossing her arms over her chest. "Do you want to talk, or not?"

"I do," he said. "Fine. Want to meet me at that bar..."

He trailed off, seeming to realize what he'd been about to say.

She frowned.

"You know the one."

"I do, Bryson."

He stared at her a few more moments. "Okay. See you there."

Gloria was shaking on the drive to the bar. She felt like there was so much at stake; at the same time, she felt as though Bryson was about to destroy her all over again.

Well...she knew that he was. He didn't want to get back together. He hadn't had a change of heart. She didn't *truly* believe that he wanted to hurt or embarrass her. He was genuinely concerned about her. He knew how badly she'd been hurt by their divorce, and how much she'd wanted to stay married.

It was just never going to make sense to her why he'd insisted upon ending it. He'd "explained" it to her, but it still seemed like bullshit.

It wasn't really because of Javier, as Bryson had continuously insisted, while they'd been together...right up until the night he'd told her—upon getting home from work, and her ready to greet him with a kiss, as she always did—that he didn't think that they could remain married.

She would never forget that feeling...disbelief, coupled with immense pain, because, deep-down, Gloria had feared—the whole time, since she'd met Bryson and they had fallen in love—that he was eventually going to leave her, because things were simply too good to be true. He was too perfect...and Gloria couldn't be *married;* it was preposterous to believe that a man would ever love her that much, to want to spend the rest of his life with her, loving her, and *only* her...

She just wasn't worth it. Before Henry, Gloria had still believed in love, and she'd believed that she would one day find a man who would love her deeply and completely, who would marry her and have babies with her.

After Henry, she'd learned that she was worthless, that she didn't have to hold out for a man who respected her, because no man ever *would.* That was just how the world was. She was a woman, so her duty was to be attractive to men and to serve them, to make the most of it when one of them stayed for a while, but to never expect too much.

Then she'd met Javier, who had taught her that love could be sincere and kind, but that it wouldn't last.

She'd thought that she finally reached absolution from her fucked up past of dating for all of the wrong reasons when she finally met Bryson, after Javier had ended their relationship. She'd trusted him. He'd asked her to move in with him and she had left her long-term apartment she shared with her best friend, and the trust had grown when he'd continued to treat her kindly and respectfully, while still giving her everything that she needed in bed, and beyond...he was the kind of dominant she hadn't believed truly existed.

Then he'd proposed, and they'd gotten married. They were even talking about trying for a baby. Then he'd come home from work that night, and he'd dropped his bomb.

"What?" she'd stammered, her lips trembling, body numb.

Bryson had stepped forward, taking hold of her shoulders. "Baby, you should sit down. We'll have to discuss this—"

"What did I do wrong?"

"Baby." He stroked her back as he walked her out of the kitchen and to the sofa, easing her down. She was shaking all over, and he looked sick as he grabbed a throw blanket off the back of the recliner and threw it over her shoulders.

"What did I do, Bryson?" she asked, tears streaming down her face.

"You haven't done anything wrong."

"Then why do you want a fucking divorce?!"

He took a deep breath. "I should have handled it better. You just looked so happy to see me...I couldn't mislead you any longer."

She started sobbing, and he got up and went to the bathroom, grabbing a box of tissues. He sat back down beside her and took her in his arms.

"I just can't do it anymore, Gloria. I never wanted to hurt you...but it's better to end it now, before you're pregnant."

Those memories that assailed Gloria as she drove to the bar, got out of her car, and waited at the entrance for Bryson, did nothing to improve her mood or to make her want to speak with him. She still felt the rawness of the pain he'd caused her, breaking her trust, destroying the happiness she'd finally allowed herself to believe in, to believe that it was meant for her, was hers for the taking, after two years of heartbreak at the hands of cruel men *and* kind, loving men.

All love was heartbreak.

He met her at the door and held it open for her. "After you."

She frowned, walking into the bar. God, they'd met there so many nights while they'd still been dating and not living together, always resulting in going back to his or her place and sleeping over.

Why had she agreed to meet him *there,* of all places? Hadn't she been through enough, without borrowing pain and willingly setting herself up to be broken?

But they made their way back to their usual booth. She ached as she sat down, but she was glad for the privacy. She had no idea what Bryson wanted to talk to her about, but she knew it couldn't be good.

He wasn't going to tell her that he wanted to get back together.

They sat and ordered drinks. Gloria ordered a Jack and Coke, and Bryson got a martini.

"Did you want to get dinner, too?" he asked.

"I'm not hungry."

"You shouldn't drink on an empty stomach."

She sighed. "I learned that in college, Bryson."

"Well..."

She frowned, lifting her eyes to his face. "It's not your job to look out for me, anymore. You're not my husband."

"I know."

They got their drinks. Gloria took a long sip of hers, then looked at Bryson. "Why did you bring me here?"

"You said you still miss me."

She swallowed. "I *do* still miss you."

"But it's not really *me* who you miss, Gloria. You miss your ex. He's the one that you wanted to be with, this whole time."

"I love you! I mean, I loved you, Bryson. You're the one who wanted a divorce. Not me."

"You never wanted to be married to *me*. You wanted to marry Javier, and he just didn't have the capacity to love you the way that I do.

"Did," Bryson said.

"Did."

"Do."

"If you still love me," Gloria began, "why did you divorce me?"

"Because I deserve to be more than a replacement for the man who didn't want to be your husband and start a family with you."

She flinched. Why was it that men she loved always knew just what to say that could hurt her the worst? And Bryson didn't even *know* about Henry.

Or Donovan...the two men who had first—and most—stolen her heart.

"I loved you," she said.

"It really hurts me worse, Gloria, that you keep saying that."

"You don't get to play the victim card with me. *You* divorced *me*. I was still in love with you."

He stared at her for a long moment. "I'm so glad that I figured this out before we got pregnant."

Tears filled her eyes.

He sighed. "Is there something that you're not telling me, Gloria?"

"I'm *not* pregnant," she whispered.

"That isn't what I meant. I'm sorry."

"Bryson..."

"I don't want you to cry."

"I miss you."

"So you've said."

"I wasn't still in love with Javier when I married you. I accepted that he didn't want the same things that I wanted...that he didn't love me how I loved him.

"You can't force those things, babe...I'm sorry. Bryson."

He swallowed. "I met him when we were together in this bar."

"I know."

"I was so happy that night. We hadn't been living together that long, but I already knew that I wanted to ask you to marry me."

"Please don't."

"But I saw the way that he looked at you, and I knew that he was still in love with you."

Gloria stared at him. "So you're saying that we got divorced over an imaginary threat?"

"No."

"*Why*, then?"

"You were there, Gloria, during the proceedings."

"Yes," she hissed. "Did you just bring me here to torture me?"

"No."

"You claimed irreconcilable differences. I said I wanted to do couples' therapy."

"I know you did."

"But I wasn't worth it to you, was I?" she asked.

"Gloria, I brought you here because I wanted to be the one to tell you...I didn't want you to find out from someone else."

"Find out what?" Gloria whispered.

He frowned. "I've got a girlfriend."

She shifted uncomfortably. "I figured you did."

"Well...she's...we're having a baby."

Her stomach dropped. Her blood ran cold. Her ears were ringing.

"Gloria."

"How...god, Bryson! You did this *today,* just to ruin the book signing for me! The one goddamned thing that I want most is what you gave to another woman."

"I didn't have sex with my girlfriend and get her pregnant in order to spite you, Gloria."

"Then why did you do it?"

It was a stupid question, Gloria knew...and she was going to get an answer that hurt her even worse.

He leaned across the table. "I've never known love like this, Gloria. It happened fast, but it's so right."

"You've never known love...Bryson. I was your wife."

"Please, don't—"

"Don't what? Be hurt? Be upset? Oh, I'm so sorry for hurting your conscience."

"Gloria, I thought that you could handle this calmly and rationally."

"Then you never fucking knew me at all, did you?"

"I didn't mean to hurt you."

"You hurt me when you asked me for a divorce. I don't think we should communicate anymore. Every time we do, you only make it worse."

"I was hoping..."

"What?" she asked, looking up at him. "That I would be happy for you, for you giving everything that I wanted to have with you, Bryson, to another woman?"

He shrugged. "Sorry. It was stupid." He started to stand up. "I should go."

"You should." She swallowed. "Wait. Let me ask you one question. It's important."

He nodded. "What?"

She took a deep breath. "Did you ever love me?"

He stared at her a few moments. "Yes, Gloria. I loved you very much."

"I loved you, too. Bryson...I still do love you."

"Please. I can't leave knowing that you're hurting so badly. I care about you, still. I wish things had worked out differently."

She smiled, but it was more of a smirk than a smile. "If that's really true, who do you love: me, or your new pregnant girlfriend?"

"Gloria...I think you know the answer to that."

She looked down into her drink. "Sure."

"Would you like another?"

"Yeah," she whispered.

She got the feeling that he wanted to chastise her on her choice to drink more on an empty stomach, but not enough to torture her further.

Instead, he nodded. "I'll have you one sent over. Gloria..."

She glanced up to meet his eyes, seeing her pain reflected back at her, in his face. She swallowed hard, despising fate in that moment...not that she'd ever truly believed in it, but fate was cruel, and easy to blame for their suffering.

"Please, allow yourself to love again. You deserve to find someone who will give you everything that you want."

"I've met plenty of perfect men. Unfortunately, I'm just not their idea of a perfect woman."

He hesitated a moment, like he wanted to say something else, but he gave up, sensing that anything he might have said would only make things worse.

So he bought her another drink, paid the bill, and left.

Gloria was stupid. She knew it was only going to make her hurt worse, but she watched him walk out of the bar.

She knew that was the last time she'd ever see her ex-husband.

It was funny...a lot of times, it was impossible to know when the last time you saw a person would be. Perhaps she should have at least felt a little closure, at that.

But she only ached worse.

Gloria downed her second Jack and Coke, fighting tears the entire time. She could only look around the bar and she was flooded by memories...memories of going home with her husband, a little bit buzzed, and him collaring her, making her crawl across the floor to him. He'd trained her, he had her performing perfectly for him.

But that hadn't been all there was to their sex life.

Gloria was adamant about keeping their BDSM play to the bedroom. Bryson had been fine with that, never making her feel as though she had to perform perfectly or do everything he wanted her to do, every time, right when he wanted it.

There had been things he'd wanted to do to her that she hadn't liked, and they'd found a compromise. Bryson liked using a belt, slapping her in the face, spitting on her...and Gloria didn't like any of those things. Instead, they'd decided she would be his pet from time to time, carrying her collar or leash to him and being naked when he came home from work.

She let him piss on her in the shower.

She'd loved him so much, and wanted to please him so desperately that she'd let him try a belt on her...it had ended disastrously, but hadn't been the end of it for them. In fact, a week later she'd moved in with him, and the level of their intimacy and trust had increased.

The sex had gotten even better.

Their love had grown deeper.

Then it had ended, as it always tended to do.

Gloria wasn't sure how she was going to get back to her apartment. She was falling apart. She could have called Cynthia, but she had already done more than enough for Gloria that day.

She knew that she even could have called Bryson, and he would have come back to take her home...but he would have done so out of guilt and pity, which she couldn't deal with right then.

But Gloria had one more person she could call...someone she wasn't one-hundred percent sure would come to her aid, but she was betting that he would.

She scrolled through her contacts and hit dial on Javier's number, barely able to hold her head up as she waited for an answer.

Or not...she was very drunk. She shouldn't have had that second drink, and she should have let Bryson buy her something to eat. Her pain and stubbornness had kept her from it.

On the fourth ring, Javier picked up. "Gloria?"

The sound of his sweet, familiar voice nearly made her weep. "Javier."

"Gloria, are you okay? What's up?"

"I'm so sorry to bother you. Are you busy?"

"No."

She swallowed hard. "Good. Fuck."

"What's wrong?"

"I need you to help me. I'm so sorry."

"What's wrong?" he repeated, impatient, stressed. "Are you okay?"

"I just need you to come and get me."

"Okay. Where are you?"

She named the bar, and she heard his exhale on the other end...the memories and nostalgia got to him the same as they did her.

They were so fucking similar.

"Okay. I'll be there in twenty minutes. Will you be okay?"

"I'm fine. I'm sitting here in a booth. I'm just...I'm falling apart."

"I'm coming."

"Thank you, Javier."

He hesitated. "Anything for you, Gloria."

True to his word, Javier arrived at the bar twenty minutes later...maybe twenty-two, but he'd hurried there, she could tell, watching him burst through the door, scanning the dimly-lit room for her.

She stood, waving to him...and he closed the distance between them so quickly, he must have crossed the room in three seconds flat.

As soon as he was in front of her, she couldn't hold back. Gloria dissolved in his arms, holding onto him fiercely.

He was right there with her, holding her close, his lips against her neck. "Are you okay?"

"I am now," she replied.

He held her a few more moments, then he carefully moved her back to the booth, sitting beside her, stroking her hair, his arm around her shoulders.

"Tell me what's wrong."

"It's a lot."

"Did you come here alone?"

She met his eyes. "No."

He grabbed a handful of bar napkins and gently dabbed at her face. "Are you hurt?"

"No, no," she said, shaking her head. "I had a book signing today."

He nodded. "I know. I wanted to come, to support you and cheer you on, but I didn't think that would be a good idea."

"Probably. I appreciate that, Javier."

"Well...I'm so happy for you."

"I know."

"So...how drunk are you, baby?"

She flinched a little...he called most women 'baby,' though...she shouldn't have thought too much of it. He lived by calling people pet names.

He'd called her 'baby' when they'd first met...

"I had two Jack and Cokes."

"And what have you eaten today?"

"A green smoothie this morning. I think I had a bagel or muffin at the signing. Don't remember which."

"So I'm ordering you some dinner."

"You don't need to do that, Javier—"

"Don't argue with me," he said.

Which shut her up immediately...

"Good girl," he whispered, stroking her hair.

She looked at him...it didn't fucking matter how much time had passed, or what either of them did. They still had that undeniable attraction to each other.

He cleared his throat. "What would you like to eat, Gloria?"

She had to bring herself back down to earth. She knew she *did* need to eat, because she felt like absolute shit.

"Um...I guess just some fries."

"I think fries sound amazing. Cheese fries?"

"You know me too well," she said.

"So, an order of cheese fries and two sodas."

She gave him the best smile she could manage...and he leaned down and kissed the top of her head, like it was the most natural thing in the world.

It made her head spin, and her heart swell, as she watched him walk away toward the bar. He was so fucking hot, definitely the sexiest man she'd ever been with. He was also the best sex, easily...even better than Henry.

Then again, sometimes she managed to convince herself that the only reason she thought Henry was a sex god was because she'd been in love with him, and because he was her first dominant.

But Javier was her healthy relationship, genuine, balanced, reciprocated love. He liked how submissive she was, but they hadn't been in a dominant/submissive relationship. They'd had plenty of kinky sex, but she had always felt as though she and Javier were more partners than anything else. He hadn't controlled her, and any time he'd denied her orgasms or spanked her, choked her, tied her up...had all been done in the name of play, completely separate from their relationship as boyfriend and girlfriend.

And he'd made love to her regularly, being sweet and gentle, making her feel loved and cherished, and—above all else—safe and secure.

She tried to relax as he made his way back to their booth, smiling at him.

He gave her a curious look. "You good, babygirl?"

"I am. I was just remembering."

He smiled. "Me too. This place is full of memories for us, isn't it?"

"The last time we were here together was when you saw me here with Bryson. Before we were engaged."

"Yeah. What happened between the two of you? I thought it was for keeps."

"So did I. Javier...Bryson caught me in the parking lot after my signing and he told me he had to talk to me...so he brought me here. And he dropped a fucking bomb."

"What did he tell you?"

Javier had his arm around her shoulder, playing with her hair as he listened attentively to her problems...he had a way of making her feel like the center of the universe when he was with her.

It was absolutely addictive.

But she felt sick as she said, "He's got a girlfriend."

"Well...that sucks, Gloria. But it happens. People move on."

"I know it," she said. "But...well, *I* haven't."

He rubbed her back. "I know, babygirl."

Sometimes Gloria had to ask herself if part of the reason she was so goddamned hot for Javier was because he called her the same names that Henry had...and they had been the only two men who had.

"But...she's having his baby..." Gloria said, looking down at her empty drink.

He wrapped his arms around her and held her against him. "I'm so sorry."

She sniffed, burying her face against his chest. She was so grateful that he was there...she had no idea what she would have done without him.

"Thank you," he said, shifting.

Gloria looked up and saw that their drinks had arrived...their sodas.

She wiped her face, and Javier got up to grab more napkins, then came back and sat beside her, wrapping his arm around her waist.

"Gloria, nothing I say is going to make this suck any less. I wish I could help you."

"It's enough that you're here."

"Well...I don't understand why he felt the need to corner you after your book signing and bring you here to tell you his news."

"I think that his intentions were good."

"You always believe that people have good intentions."

She reached down and took his hand, holding it in both of hers...she felt as though he was the only thing that she had left to hold onto. She knew it wasn't fair. He didn't want to be with her. They'd broken up.

He was there out of the kindness of his heart, and because that was the kind of a person that he was, and because he'd loved her once. He wasn't the type to move on as though nothing had ever happened.

"He said he didn't want me to hear it from someone else," she said.

He reached out to cup her cheek in one hand, dabbing her tears away with his other. She saw a shadow cross his face, and she knew he was furious with Bryson...it hadn't taken much.

She knew that Javier had never liked Bryson, which she'd always found amusing, because they were really similar...except that Bryson was rich and Javier wasn't. She had to believe that part of the reason that Javier disliked Bryson so much was because he thought that Bryson could give Gloria a life that he couldn't have...and that he didn't think Bryson deserved the money he had.

It was stupid. Javier had broken up with Gloria, and it had nothing to do with money.

"Fuck him. You always deserved better."

She laughed. "It's so stupid. Two perfect, loving relationships in a row, and I lost them both."

"You didn't lose anything, babygirl. Two men lost a good woman."

"Why did you break up with me, then, Javier?"

He stroked her hair. "You know why."

She swallowed. "Do I, though?"

"Our relationship never could have lasted."

She took a sip of her soda, trying to dislodge the smothering lump in her throat.

"Hey...I'm not trying to make it worse for you, baby."

"You could never hurt me," she said, softly. She gave his hand a squeeze. "God, it was wonderful while it lasted, wasn't it, though?"

"Yours is the best love I've ever known. If I didn't think that it would destroy you, then I'd suggest we remain friends with benefits."

She smiled, sadly. "It would definitely destroy me."

"Which is why I never offered, or asked."

Their food came, and Javier handed her the ketchup bottle, knowing she loved to drench every fry in as much of the sweet red sauce as possible.

He watched her take a small bite of the fries. "You're so beautiful."

She laughed. "Thank you. I needed that."

They didn't speak for the first few minutes, both eating the cheese fries, Javier occasionally stroking her thigh or back as they ate...it was like he couldn't keep his hands off of her.

He never could, when they'd been together.

"Javier..." she began, wiping her fingers clean, hesitating because she knew she was a little drunk and she didn't need to ask him what she wanted to ask. "Why?"

He stared at her. "Really?"

She nodded.

"Well, let me ask you, babygirl...who did you think about when you were laying beside me in bed and touched yourself, when you thought I was asleep?"

"I didn't—"

"Did I not get you off?"

"That's not why you broke up with me," Gloria said, weakly.

"No, we broke up because I don't want kids, and you do. No matter how you insisted that you would give up having a family for me, we both know that, every few months, you'd start on me again."

"I wanted you to be happy."

"I loved you, Javier."

"And I badly hurt you."

"I got hurt," she whispered.

"You know I'm not the man you loved. You would never be satisfied with me...I was so jealous of Bryson. But now I know you did him the same way.

"Who was he, Gloria? You said his name at least three times when I was fucking you."

She looked at him. "You counted?"

He nodded.

"Fuck," she said, putting her head in her hands. "I really did hurt you. I'm so sorry."

"Well, we hurt each other." He shrugged. "You didn't do it on purpose."

"God, I loved you. I didn't think I would ever get over you."

It hurt her stomach to think that she'd hurt him by saying Henry's name during sex, the same way he'd hurt her when they'd broken up.

"Are you going to eat the rest of your fries?" he asked. "You need to soak up as much of that alcohol as you can."

"Yes, Javier."

He moved his hand up her back, to the back of her neck...his fingers slightly tightened around her neck, and—even as she sat there heartbroken—she instantly got wet, thinking about how good he was in bed.

She wondered how it would be to fuck him one last time, for some closure...at least, she *told* herself that was why she wanted to fuck him.

"Javier."

He clearly knew what she was thinking. He frowned. "Who the fuck is Henry, baby-girl?"

Gloria couldn't have explained why she reacted as she did, to that...with the exception of figuring it had something to do with the fact that she felt defensive when it came to Henry, like she still had that same sick obsession she'd had before, with protecting him.

The other was that she didn't want to admit that Henry still had any power over her.

"You hurt me, Javier, so terribly," Gloria said. "And you want to try to blame me for our breakup? I mourned you for *months.*"

"You were a wreck, I know it," Javier said.

"Because I was devastated, losing you. I loved you so much."

"You never answered my question. Who is Henry?"

She looked down at the table. "My first dominant."

"Oh."

She swallowed. "Yeah."

"Gloria, I loved you, too. I truly did love you. But we were never meant to last."

She gasped.

"Please," Javier said.

"What, you don't want to see how badly you've hurt me? You don't want to admit that you're not the victim, for fucking once?"

He stared at her for a long moment, frowning. She knew she'd taken it too far, calling him out on his deepest insecurities.

She breathed out. "Fuck. Javier, I'm sorry."

"I know. It's okay, babe."

"No, it isn't." She looked up at him. "I'm sorry. It's just...we ended. But the reason that Bryson divorced me is because he's convinced that you and I are still in love."

"In another lifetime, baby," he said.

"I felt so safe with you."

"I hate seeing you hurting. As much as I hated the thought of you being with another man, I was glad that you found someone who was good to you."

"Javier."

"What?"

She sighed. "I know that we can't be together. But I don't want to be alone tonight. Can I stay with you?"

He nodded. "Of course you can."

Javier drove her car to his house, because she was too distraught and too drunk.

"What about your car?"

"A couple of my buddies are just down the road. One of them will drop it off at my place. I arranged that on the drive over."

"You're too good."

"I'm a piece of shit, babygirl, you've just got a soft spot for me."

"Bullshit," she whispered, settling in her passenger seat, slowly relaxing...she almost felt as though she were floating. She was drunk, but the cheese fries felt good in her belly...or maybe it was being in close quarters—alone—with her lover again.

"I looked for any excuse I could find to be with you," he said, "even when I knew I needed to stay away from you."

She flinched. It still hurt, thinking about those weeks, then months, after Javier, being alone, remembering how nice it had been to sleep in his bed, or to have him in her bed, how she never slept well when they couldn't sleep over at each other's houses. When she finally felt as though she was safe to love again.

He parked her car on the street in front of his house, then came around to the passenger side to help her out. He wrapped his arm around her waist, holding her tight, her handbag over his other arm as he walked her to his house.

He took her into his house and sat her in the armchair. "Can I get you some water?"

She nodded. "Thank you, babe."

He came back and handed her the water.

Then he went and sat across the coffee table from her, watching her as she took a sip.

"Thank you, Javier."

"It almost feels right, doesn't it?" he asked, looking at her.

She stood and moved to sit on the sofa beside him, putting her arms around him. He pulled her close to him, letting her lay her head on his chest.

He rubbed her back as he held her; she felt so safe. It was such a familiar feeling to be in his arms in his home that she started crying.

She couldn't help it.

"Oh, fuck, Gloria," he said, stroking her back. "Please don't cry."

"It's not your fault," she cried, reaching up to rub the back of his neck as he held her. "I'm just broken. You're not the one who did it to me. You only tried to love me."

"I did love you."

"I know," she whispered.

He kissed the top of her head, then...and it made her melt.

She reached up to take his face in her hands, looking at him.

He leaned his head down and softly kissed her, his tenderness making her stomach twist viciously.

She moaned as he grabbed the back of her neck, deepening their kiss. He eased her lips apart as he worked his mouth against hers, his tongue inside her mouth.

He lifted her into his lap, and she wrapped her arms and legs around him, grinding her hips against him, arching her back.

He put his mouth against her neck. "Do you want to go to my bedroom?"

"Yes," she sighed, slipping off of his lap.

He stood and took her hand, taking her back to his bedroom.

It was a surreal feeling, being in his bedroom again.

She had been happy the last time they'd been there; he had broken up with her at *her* apartment, the one she'd lived in with Cynthia, when Cynthia and her boyfriend now lived.

But the *last time* she'd been in Javier's bed, she had been so happy, so in love. They'd made love for hours...each time they finished, she would lie against his chest, and he would kiss her and tell her that he loved her. She would rest her head on his chest, sleep in his arms for a while...

Then she would wake up and they would fuck, all over again.

She jumped when she felt Javier's hand against the small of her back, guiding her into his room.

"I'm sorry, he said, kissing the back of her neck. "I didn't mean to startle you."

"I was just...remembering."

"Baby. I know," he said, gently turning her in his arms, to face him.

She smiled up at him, but she saw her own sadness reflected back at her, in her eyes.

They both knew *that* time, that it was the last time they would be together. It would end, as soon as she left in the morning...

"Tonight," she said, "it's only the two of us. We won't think about what will happen in the morning.

"Tonight, we can be in love."

"I never stopped loving you, Gloria."

"I know it. I spent months getting over you."

He held her close, kissing her slowly, deeply, possessively, like she was his again.

Like he owned her.

She moaned. "Oh, *fuck,* Javier."

He responded by reaching down, cupping her butt in his hands, and squeezing her tightly. She pressed her body firmly against him, reaching down to lift his t-shirt.

"Okay," he said, yanking his shirt off over his head, tossing it aside.

Gloria moaned, stroking his chest, loving the feel of his chest hair against her fingers. ..she traced his tattoos, dying to feel his hairy chest against her bare skin, something she'd missed for so long...

She reached up and kissed him, softly...she wanted him, yes, and desperately, but she wanted it to be slow, sweet, and soft. She hadn't had sex since the night before Bryson had told her he wanted a divorce. She had convinced herself that she wasn't in the mood, but all of her hormones she'd put on hold had gone rogue the second she'd kissed Javier.

She could think of little else but being naked in his bed, again.

He cupped the back of her neck in his hand, pressing his lips more insistently against hers. She whimpered as he moved one hand to her breasts, squeezing her right breast, hard.

"Fuck."

"Too hard?" he asked, his lips still against hers.

She could taste his breath in her mouth, the cheese fries, the soda.

She wanted more of his touch. Desperately.

"No," she whispered.

He tried to undress her, but struggled with the straps and hooks. "How the fuck do you get this thing off, baby?"

She laughed, pressing her lips against his briefly before pulling away, smiling at him. "It's a jumpsuit."

"I'm not fancy enough for that shit."

"Oh, you've never made love to a woman who wore one of these? I thought you'd had dozens of lovers, Javier."

"Jealous?"

She met his eyes. "You know I am."

"I'm yours, Gloria. Now, take off that suit and let me see you. It's been way too long."

Her hands shook as she undid the clasps up the front of her suit, her stomach in knots...it was anticipation, she knew. She had no reason to be nervous around Javier. He'd seen every inch of her body, and had her in every way imaginable. What was more, the two of them had no secrets.

He reached out to grab her wrist in his hand. "Are you okay, baby?"

She nodded. "Just a little nervous. I've not had sex in a while."

He stepped closer, still holding her wrist. "It's okay, we can take things as slowly as you need us to."

"Yes, Javier," she whispered, her voice trembling.

He kissed her as he reached down to gently finish unfastening her jumpsuit, then he leaned in and kissed her neck as he eased the suit off her shoulders.

She felt the slinky fabric slip down her hips and land in a heap on the floor. Her legs were shaking, so she wrapped her arms around his shoulders and held onto him before her knees gave out.

He licked her throat as he reached down to cup her butt in his hands again, trailing his thumbs over her soft skin and her round ass.

She moaned, leaning her head back and running her fingers through his hair. "Fuck. I love you, Javier."

"I love you, babygirl," he replied, running his mouth down her neck, to her breasts. He licked the soft flesh over the top of her lacy bra. "God, you're so fucking gorgeous. Better than I remembered."

She smiled. He always knew just what to say to make her feel better.

He stepped closer, lifting her into his arms. She wrapped her arms and legs around him and he carried her to his bed, lying her down gently.

She sat up on her elbows, watching him as he stood over her, seemingly like he couldn't decide if he wanted to lie down with her and kiss her, or if he wanted to strip off his own clothes first.

She leaned forward. "Come here, Javier."

He stepped forward within her reach. She smiled up at him, then she reached to the fly of his pants, unzipping and working his jeans down his hips, moaning softly at the sight of his erection through his underwear.

She wanted his cock in her mouth, or—better yet—shoved down her throat.

She stroked him through his briefs, teasing him, wondering if she could get him turned-on enough to turn the red fabric over his cock slightly darker with precum.

"Gloria," he said.

"Get in bed with me, babe."

She scooted back so that he could climb in between her legs, positioning himself to take her.

He lowered himself over her, kissing her breasts, then up her neck—slowly—before he put his mouth back on hers, licking her lips before taking her mouth, claiming her as his.

He slowly ran his hands down her body as he kissed her, around her back to unsnap her bra. He moved back down her body, licking her nipples, making her nearly come off the bed.

She moaned. "I love you."

"I love you, babygirl," he repeated, sucking her left nipple as he cupped her right breast. "I fucking love you."

She reached down to cup him, over his underwear. "I love your cock. I've missed it."

"It's missed you too, babygirl."

"Show me," she said.

He flipped her over onto her belly, grabbing her hair in one hand. He bent over her and kissed, then bit, her neck, lightly.

Then he sat back, pushing her legs apart. He dropped her hair so that he could yank down her panties, shoving his face between her buttcheeks as soon as he had her naked.

She moaned as he ate her ass, sniffing her, licking her butthole, easing his tongue inside her as he reached inside her with his fingers, instantly finding her g-spot as his tongue continued caressing and teasing her butthole.

"Javier," she whimpered.

"You like it when I eat your ass, don't you, babygirl?"

"Fucking love it," she whimpered. "Please."

But he flipped her over again, sitting on his knees over her. As she watched, he sucked his fingers he'd had inside her.

She moaned, spreading her thighs and arching her back.

"Do you want me inside you?"

"Yes," she whispered.

He pulled down his underwear and tossed it aside. God, he had the perfect cock. Not so long as it was thick, but plenty long enough to fuck her hard.

And thick enough to stretch her so wide that her legs shook, and that she begged him to be more gentle...which he had.

Sometimes.

She reached forward to touch him...god, he felt incredible, so hard and ready to take her. She looked into his eyes as she stroked him, easing her hand up and down his shaft, holding his tip between her thumb and the rest of her fingers, rubbing around his slit.

She knew him so well, so intimately. Deeply. She knew what turned him on, and she knew exactly how he loved to be touched.

She smiled as she watched him coming apart beneath her touch. She longed to make him lose control, to remind him of what they'd had together.

How perfect it had been, how perfect the two of them were for each other...

He reached forward and wrapped his hand around her neck. "Lie back, babygirl. I'm going to put my dick inside you."

She moaned, lying back and lifting her hips, eagerly awaiting him making good on his promise.

He positioned himself over her, between her legs, to take her...then he paused.

"Do I need a condom?"

"I only slept with Bryson. He was faithful to me."

"But, are you...I mean."

She shook her head. "We were talking about it, but I never stopped taking my pill."

"Good," he said, gripping her breasts as he kissed her neck, easing inside her. "I would hate not to feel your tight cunt around me, raw."

She whimpered as he thrust deep inside her, circling his hips so that he rubbed all inside her, in her most sensitive areas. She arched her back and pushed up against him, grinding her hips in time with his. He moved faster, fucking her harder and harder. She was gasping and whimpering as he relentlessly kept on fucking her, grabbing her hips and holding her tightly against him. He pumped away at her...if he'd had a long dick, he might have destroyed her.

She would have welcomed his destruction.

She rose higher, knowing she was close, but wanting to hold on longer. She hadn't had an orgasm in so long—it had been even longer since she'd had one with a man inside her—that she wanted it to last, wanted it to be perfect and she wanted them to get off together...she wanted him to shoot his cum inside her at the same time that she started throbbing around him, as her cervix rose and as her body welcomed his seed...god, she wanted that.

"Baby," she whispered, barely hanging on.

"What is it?" he asked, reaching down between their sweaty bodies to grab and twist her nipple.

She moaned, then cried out as he choked her, then as he grabbed her tighter, his thighs and stomach slapping against hers as he fucked her even faster.

"Ugh, it hurts," she said, the skin around her vagina pinching from all of the friction.

"Harder, did you say?" Javier asked.

She moaned as he choked and fucked her harder...then slowly, he let up.

She knew he hadn't cum inside her yet. She was confused, and she moaned in protest as he gently settled on top of her.

"Javier."

"You said I was hurting you, babygirl." He looked at her tenderly, reaching out to brush her hair out of her face.

She swallowed. "I don't mind."

He smiled. "Sweet girl."

"I love you. I need you. I need you to finish."

He stroked her cheek. "I plan to do just that, beautiful."

She wrapped her legs around his waist, forcing him deeper inside her. "Finish inside me," she said, cupping the back of his neck in her hand.

In response, he took her face in his hands, kissing her deeply as he began moving inside her again, slowly, steadily. He gave her the chance to figure out his rhythm, then she began moving with him, pushing back against him as he thrust.

She moaned as he kissed her, as he tightened his grip on her neck.

He kissed her, then put his mouth beside her ear as he thrust, and said, "I've missed fucking you, Gloria. You're the best sex I've ever had."

She whimpered as he continued fucking her...god, he knew how to fuck her, how to choke her, and just the right combination of the two, where she felt desperate just as she started to come, that light-headedness overcoming her as her orgasm washed over her...

He licked her neck, then said, "You're so fucking tight, I know just when you're getting ready to come. You're a nasty little whore, aren't you? When I was eating your ass, you wanted it to be my cock inside you, instead of my tongue. Isn't that right, babygirl?"

Her breathing got shallower, heavier, as she got closer, feeling the tingles in her back, in her breasts, in her head.

Then he hit deeper, still slow and gentle, and she knew she was coming.

As he pressed inside her, he said, "Don't worry, baby. I'll fuck your ass as much as you want me to, tonight."

Her pants became soft whimpers as her orgasm washed over her, her vision getting grey. She felt his cum shooting up inside her, heard his groans as he came.

Her whimpers became moans, then cries, over and over as she gave herself to the sensation washing over her. She shook, clinging to his back as she held him.

Her body jerked hard, then, at the continued sensation. She writhed beneath him. "Fuck, Javier!"

He laughed, easing off of her. He kept himself buried inside her, though, flexing his hips to make her whimper again.

"Javier."

"It's alright, baby," he said, stroking her sides as he eased his body down beside hers, still holding her in his arms.

She kept her left leg hooked over his hip as he held her, as they settled in each other's arms, coming down from such an intense orgasm.

She sighed, and it came out as a whimper. "God."

"That was better than I remember."

She smiled at him. "Me, too."

"Why did I break up with you?" he asked, sounding truly remorseful.

"I have no idea."

"I do. It's just hard to remember when I've got you in my bed, again."

She sighed. "I know."

"I don't want to hurt you."

"I don't want to be hurt."

He reached down and touched her breast, looking into her eyes. "Well, it's too late to not sleep together."

"I wouldn't trade what just happened to not be hurt."

"You're sweet, Gloria, and you're loving. You've got a tender heart. You need someone who can give you the love you want...and everything else that goes along with it."

"Thank you," she whispered.

But brokenly.

"Babygirl, don't be sad. Remember, we're happy tonight. You're mine, and I'm yours."

"Yes, Javier."

He kissed her. "I love you. No matter what. I'm always going to love you, and a part of me will always be in love with you."

"Me, too."

She settled against his chest, and he stroked her hair, then down her back. Over and over, until she felt her body start to relax.

"I feel so safe with you."

"You are safe with me," he said.

She fell asleep, and she woke up maybe half an hour later, and Javier was still holding her.

She looked up at him, and the way that he looked at her made her heart lurch. She swallowed, forcing her emotions down.

She didn't want to destroy a wonderful night by focusing on how hard it would be to leave him in the morning.

She ran her fingers over his chest. "I forgot how hot you are."

He laughed. "Thank you."

"Definitely the hottest guy I ever fucked."

He kissed her. "You're the most beautiful woman I've ever slept with."

"Am I?"

"Of course you are, baby." He tightened his arms around her. "Now, let's see about fucking that asshole, do you think?"

She smiled. "I could be persuaded."

"Persuaded? You'll be begging me to take your asshole within the next three minutes, I guarantee you."

"Show me."

He took her face in his hands, putting his mouth on hers.

She moaned softly, relaxing in his arms at the same time as she was getting incredibly turned on, her butthole throbbing at the idea of him slipping his cock inside it. She rolled onto her stomach, spreading her legs for him.

He positioned himself behind her, smacking her butt, making her moan. "You're so fucking good, babe."

"Don't get ahead of yourself, babygirl. I'm not putting my dick in you until you're good and ready." He rubbed her butt gently.

"Yes, Javier."

He slapped her ass again, then he leaned down and gently kissed the red spot his hand had left.

She moaned.

"I'm going to put my cock in your throat."

She nodded, turning to face him. He got on his knees on his bed, and he held his dick in one hand as he moved closer to her.

Eagerly, she took him in her mouth, holding his gaze as she worked her mouth over the head of his cock, licking him, then sucking him slowly deeper into her mouth, until his tip was at the back of her throat.

He took her face in his hands, like he was going to be gentle and tender, then he pushed himself deep into her throat.

She'd been prepared, and she'd had a lot of practice since Henry. She took him, no problem.

She held onto his hips, drawing him closer, deeper into her throat, breathing carefully through her nose. She held his gaze as he carefully thrust into her throat. He was so much more gentle than most men she'd been with, while still being in control and pleasing her sexually.

Which fed her heart, fed her emotionally.

He flexed his hips, making her whimper as she kept her throat open, taking him in over and over as he gave measured, cautious thrusts, to fuck her face while still being considerate of her comfort. That was one of the things that she adored most about Javier...well, about *fucking* Javier...that he was gentle and he cared, and he knew that treating her that way made her want him even more, and made her more and more willing to be slutty for him.

He knew how it worked, and he knew how to work her.

He didn't cum in her throat, though. He eased out of her, and he sat in front of her, kissing her.

She put her hands around the back of his neck, caressing him as he kissed her. His lips were so gentle, and he was so full of passion.

The only time Bryson had kissed her that way was when he'd been fucking her, or after he'd pinned her down in the shower, fucked her hard, and pissed on her...which she'd enjoyed, and she'd known that he loved her, he loved her all the time, no matter what it was that the two of them were doing together. But the only time he gave her that level of tenderness and passion was when he'd done something depraved to her.

She forced thoughts of Bryson from her mind as she moaned into Javier's mouth, kissing him harder, her lips clinging desperately to his as she worked her mouth on his.

She moaned again. "I love you, Javier."

He raked his fingers through her hair, reaching down to slip his fingers inside her. She gasped, arching her back, driving his fingers deeper inside her.

"Easy, babygirl. I don't want to hurt you."

"I don't mind," she whispered.

"Well, I do." He rubbed her g-spot in deep, slow strokes, then he pulled his fingers out and wrapped them around her throat.

"Mmm, yes," she moaned.

"Easy," Javier cautioned, leaning over her to kiss her again, as he choked her.

He flipped her over. "On your hands and knees, babygirl, okay?"

"Yes, Javier."

"Good girl." He positioned himself between her legs again, licking her butthole, making her tremble beneath his tongue.

"After I'm done fucking your ass, we're taking a shower together," he said. "So I can fuck your tight cunt again later."

"Yes, Javier," she repeated.

He slapped her butt, which was getting red and raw from all the smacks he'd been giving her...in turn, making her even wetter.

He sank his teeth into the soft skin of her ass, making her cry out in pain, then he kissed her gently over the marks he'd left on her.

"Javier, I—"

"Shh."

She bit down on her lower lip as he turned his attention back to her butthole, licking her, easing his fingers inside her vagina, rubbing her, making her push back against him, desperate for more of his touch, for him to never stop.

She arched her back as he kept licking her butthole and fingering her. After a few more moments, he eased his index finger inside her butt, rubbing her gently.

Then he began stroking her vaginal walls and her anus simultaneously. She whimpered as he got her closer and closer to coming, then he removed his fingers from her vagina entirely, sinking three of his fingers into her butthole, stretching her.

"Please, Javier," she whimpered.

"Do you want me to fuck your asshole, babygirl?"

She reached back to hold her cheeks wide open, looking over her shoulder at him, biting her lip. "Please, babe."

"Anything my babygirl wants, she gets," he said, taking himself in his hand, holding himself outside her entrance.

"Yes, Javier."

He slowly eased himself inside her, being gentle. She whimpered a little at the pain, but she relaxed as he stroked her back, welcoming him inside her.

He pushed inside deeper. Once he got in past his tip, it was much easier for her to take him with enthusiasm.

He thrust inside her once, twice.

"I love you, Javier."

He moaned as he kept fucking her. She sucked in a breath...it wasn't particularly painful, but she needed a little more...

He read her mind then, as he always could. He reached in front and began rubbing circles over her as he kept fucking her butt.

"Javier," she whimpered.

He grabbed her hips firmly, slapping into her hard, as he was close to coming...close to filling her butthole with his cum.

She pushed back against him, and he groaned as he spilled his cum inside her.

He held her hips, still. He kissed the back of her neck, then reached up—with the hand he'd been rubbing her clit with—and he gripped her breasts, twisting her nipples, making her squirm.

"Good girl," he said. "God, I've missed this."

"Me, too." She looked over her shoulder at him. "Nobody makes me feel this way. You're the only one."

"That's because you're my soulmate, babygirl."

She smiled up at him, then flipped over onto her back, pulling him down on top of her.

He pressed his forehead against hers. "God, I am in love with you, babygirl. How couldn't I be? You're everything I ever wanted in a lover."

"Then make me yours," she said.

"I think that's what I just did, isn't it?" he asked, brushing her hair gently back from her face.

"Javier, I meant that—"

"I know what you meant." He leaned down to kiss her softly. "But we agreed that we weren't going to discuss that tonight, didn't we?"

She swallowed. "Yes, Javier."

"Good girl." He kissed her again. "That's my baby."

She whimpered.

He eased off of her, sitting back, between her legs again.

She sat up on her elbows again, looking at him.

He pushed her legs apart and touched her. She moaned, but he pushed up, and she lifted her hips.

"I want to see my cum pouring out of your asshole, babygirl."

She spread her cheeks, and he moaned as she gaped her asshole for him, so that he could see inside her.

Then she clenched her hole, and he groaned as his cum spilled out of her. "Good girl. Fuck, Gloria. You're fucking hot."

"Come here," she told him.

He eased her legs down, then slowly moved back up her body, until he was pressed against her and in her arms.

She sighed happily, holding him close as she rubbed his back and kissed his hair. She knew it in her soul that it wasn't only their intense sexual connection that had them addicted to each other; she loved him, and he loved her.

They were in love.

And they couldn't last. They'd tried it, and they'd hurt each other, but, god...coming together that night, after everything that had happened, was almost more than her mind could comprehend. He was going to leave scars all over her heart, and she would never really know how to go on without him.

But she wasn't going to spoil what they *did* have, there, together, that night, by fearing what would happen in the morning, when she went home, and when they likely never saw each other again.

The thought of it sent a pang through her. Gloria gasped, sitting up.

"Baby, what's wrong?"

She covered her mouth as she hurried out of his bedroom and down the hallway to his bathroom.

She barely got the toilet seat lifted before she vomited into it.

She choked and gasped for breath, and Javier knelt in the floor with her, holding her hair back. "You're okay, babygirl."

"I'm sorry."

He rubbed her back. "It's okay."

She barely held back a sob. He tenderly played with her hair. "What's going on, Gloria?"

She reached for the toilet paper, pulling off a few sheets to wipe her mouth and her eyes. "I'm so sorry. I just...I lost it."

"Did I hurt you?"

"No. God, no, babe. Tonight is so perfect."

"Is it the alcohol?"

She nodded, not meeting his eyes. "That must be it."

"Tell me the truth, Gloria."

"I just...I thought about leaving here in the morning."

He sighed. "Of course you did."

She started crying harder.

He held her close, rubbing her back. "I never should have slept with you tonight."

"Yes! Tonight has been incredible, Javier. I don't regret a single thing that we've done together. It's been the happiest I've felt in ages."

"Don't think for a second that it's going to be any easier for me to let you go in the morning. I'm going to miss you for the rest of my life."

"Then why the fuck are we going our separate ways? Maybe this was meant to happen, to show us both that we've got to be together."

He shook his head. "I won't be responsible for breaking your heart again."

"Then let me break my own heart."

"No."

"Javier, I need you."

"I need you too. But it doesn't matter. We tried this. We don't belong together. Soulmates or not, we're not meant to be."

"Yes, we are."

He sighed, reaching down to wrap his fingers around her neck. "I'll fuck you all night if you want me to, but I won't promise you forever. I'll never be able to offer you that."

"You're not a liar."

"No. I'm not."

She held his gaze, her vision blurred by the tears pooling in her eyes.

"Come here," he said, pulling her back into his arms, cradling her face against his chest.

She wrapped her arms around him, holding him tightly.

He let her cry, then. But Gloria didn't want to waste the night crying, when she could have been spending it in his arms for a completely different reason.

She swallowed her tears and pulled away, her hands on his muscular forearms.

He met her eyes, concern etched in every line of his face...along with dread.

She smiled, softly. "I'm sorry. I'll pull it together, babe."

"I feel like I'm hurting you."

"I'm hurting myself. It's fine, you saved me tonight."

"Promise me."

She reached forward and cupped his cheek in her hand. "I promise you, my love."

He leaned in and kissed her gently...slowly pulling her closer. She ended up in his lap, wrapped around him, beginning to grind her hips against him as she felt his erection against her thigh.

She smiled against his mouth, sighing as she reached down and took him into her hand, making him moan.

"You're mine," she said, pulling away from kissing him so that she could look into his eyes. "Your cock belongs to me, Javier."

He cupped her chin. "Should I get your name tattooed on it, babygirl?"

"So that everyone you sleep with from this day onward knows that they're only getting to borrow your cock for a while?" She smiled. "Be my guest."

He reached down, then, taking her left hand in his, stroking the inside of her ring finger, where her black heart—though faded after two years—was still there, still visible.

"I'll tattoo your name on my cock if you tell me what this tattoo means."

"Of all the tattoos I've got on my body, this is the one you want to ask me about?" she asked, smiling a little.

"Well, the butterfly on your ass is gorgeous, but I've got a hard time believing that it means much of anything, other than that you like doggy-style."

"It's my favorite."

"I know, babygirl," he said, reaching out to touch her left nipple.

She moaned softly, pushing into his hand. "God."

"How about we get in the shower? Are you feeling better?"

She nodded. "Can I brush my teeth?"

He helped her to her feet. "Your toothbrush is under my sink."

It made her almost get choked up again, thinking about him still having her toothbrush at his place, even though they'd broken up over a year ago. It was like he'd held onto the idea that they would be together, that she'd be sleeping over at his house again.

She brushed her teeth while he started the shower. She rinsed her mouth...she wasn't sure what to do with the toothbrush, but she didn't have it in her heart to do anything other than put it right back under the sink, beside a box of her favorite brand of tampons.

She straightened up and turned to face him, and he was looking at her in a way that made her knees weak.

"I love you," she whispered.

He held out his hand. "Come here, babygirl."

She did, pressing against his chest as he enveloped her in his arms. She sighed, reaching up to run her fingers through his hair.

She never wanted to forget how she felt in that moment, standing naked in his bathroom, wrapped in his arms, feeling his hairy chest against her nude body, his strong arms around her waist...

She looked up at him. "I fucking love you. I'm in love with you."

"Come in the shower with me," he said, taking her hand as he stepped in.

She did, and he angled her under the spray of the showerhead. She looked at him as the water covered her, and he reached out, taking her by her neck, and gently pulling her closer as he leaned in to kiss her.

"It doesn't bother you to kiss me after I vomited?"

He laughed. "You kissed me after I ate your ass."

She smiled. "Right."

He kissed her then, pulling her against him, deepening the kiss, slipping his tongue into her mouth, running his hand down to her butt, spreading her cheeks and fingering her butthole. She moaned.

"Too much?" he asked, smacking her ass.

She smiled. "No."

"Turn around, babygirl."

She did, putting her hands against the fiberglass walls of his shower, arching her back. She wanted him to take her.

He pressed his body against her, his hands over hers, against the wall. He laced his fingers through hers as he put his mouth on the back of her neck.

She whimpered as she felt his lips against her skin.

"Oh, would you rather me bite you?"

She moaned. "Fuck. You can do anything you want to me, baby."

He kissed her neck slowly.

He wanted the night to last, wanted to make the most of every moment...he maybe even wanted to do it so slowly so that they'd have time to realize that—no matter what either of them believed or what the past had told them—they belonged together.

"I'm going to make you so sore you can't sit down for days." He licked her jawline.

She laughed. "No you're not. You're too sweet for that."

"I'm whatever you want me to be tonight, babygirl," he said.

"Then put your cock inside me and fuck me from behind like you told me you would," Gloria said, looking over her shoulder at him. Then he met her mouth with his.

She moaned as he gave her a long, possessive kiss. She arched her back harder, aching for him to take her like he'd promised he would.

"I need you," she whispered, meeting his eyes.

"You have me. I'm all yours, babygirl."

He took his right hand off of hers and reached down to ease himself inside her; Gloria used her free hand to put her hand behind his neck, looking into his eyes as he entered her... then her eyes rolled back in her head.

He just had that effect on her, every goddamn time they fucked.

He slowly stretched her, increasing his pace as she pushed back, whimpering at the feel of him inside her.

He reached around her front, between her legs, and started rubbing her clit. With his other hand, he reached up to wrap his fingers around her neck.

She braced herself with one hand and reached back with her other, holding him against her as he pounded away at her.

He put his mouth against her neck. "After I cum inside your cunt, babygirl, I'm going to have you suck me off.

"Then before I let you rest, I'm taking you back to the bedroom, bending you over the edge of my bed, and I'm going to fill you again."

She whimpered, as she rode higher and higher. "Are you close, baby?"

"Yes," he choked out.

She moaned, pushing back, meeting his every thrust. She got louder, crying out as she started to come, throbbing around his cock as she milked him.

"Fuck, Gloria," he moaned, holding her hips as he pounded at her, finishing off.

Her legs shook so hard she could barely stand up.

He turned her around, holding her in his arms as he looked down at her like he was in love with her.

She nodded, cupping the back of his neck in her hand as she looked up into his eyes. She could love a million other men in her life, and none of them would touch her heart quite the same way that Javier had, with his sensual mixture of sweetness and his insatiable—sometimes depraved—appetite for sex.

She sucked in a breath, forcing down her regrets as she took his mouth with hers. She kissed him like the world was ending, like the only thing that mattered was him, her love for him, and showing him just how much he meant to her.

Everything.

He put his hands on her shoulders and gently eased her onto the shower floor. She knelt obediently, looking up at him, never taking her eyes off of him.

She took him in her mouth, the taste of his cum so familiar to her, comforting. Then again, most cum tasted the same, she figured...she was romanticizing it.

She didn't care. Anything to make their last night together more special.

She sucked him off, with gentle touching, stroking the back of his legs, licking and sucking him, not taking him too deeply, being soft and loving.

He pulled her to her feet and took her in his arms. "You're amazing, Gloria."

She sighed. "So are you."

He held her a few more moments, then he reached behind him and turned off the water. She looked up at him, her wet hair falling in front of her face. She took a deep breath, and he cupped her face in his hands. "I love you."

"I love you. God, I fucking love you. I'm always going to love you."

"I know." He kissed her head. "Me, too."

She nodded.

He stared at her a few more moments, then he stepped back. "Come on."

He got out of the shower, then, holding his hands out to her. He helped her out, and he grabbed her a towel to wrap in.

He stepped closer to her, taking her face in his hands again. "Okay. I'm going to make some coffee. Want some?"

"Yes."

He kissed her again. "Don't get dressed. I have a sweatshirt you can wear. I want to go outside and drink coffee and talk. Okay?"

She nodded. "Perfect."

"You know where my closet is. Help yourself."

He left the bathroom. Gloria looked under the sink and found her old hairbrush she'd left there...god, the more things that she found, the more it hurt to see how many pieces of their life together that he'd held onto.

It made her think that he was as unhappy without her as she was without him.

She combed her hair and dried it a little with a towel, then she wrapped the towel back around her waist and went to his bedroom.

His closet was against the far wall, on the opposite side of his bed. She found a sweatshirt that she pulled on, that fell to her upper thighs. She didn't feel like putting the fancy panties on again, so she left them off as she went to the kitchen to find him.

He was brewing the coffee, leaning over the kitchen counter, reading a magazine he had sitting out.

She went to stand beside him.

"Are you okay?" he asked.

She leaned against his side as he put his arm around her. "I'm wonderful."

"I just thought the coffee might help with your inevitable hangover."

She smiled. "You just want me to be up all night."

He kissed her. "You know me."

She held his gaze. "Yeah, I do."

He seemed to know that there was a deeper meaning behind her words. Yes, she knew him, but he couldn't let her get too comfortable, or she wouldn't leave in the morning...it was such a fine line to walk, and her balance was precarious at the best of times.

That night, Gloria was far from being at her best.

They went outside with mugs of coffee, once it finished brewing. He sat on the back porch, and she sat beside him. He wrapped his arm around her shoulder, holding her close to him. Perhaps he only meant to keep her warm, but they both knew better than to believe that.

She took a sip. He'd had to put a lot of milk in hers, because she hated the taste of coffee...and it reminded her of Henry, even though it had been two years since she'd even spoken to him, and millions of people drank coffee.

There was nothing about coffee that should have been exclusive to Henry.

"I only like coffee when you make it," she said, looking up at him.

He smiled. "You also only like anal when I give it to you."

She laughed. "Oh, fuck." She smiled at him. "You always know just what to say to me."

"I thought we should talk," he said, his tone growing slightly more serious. "I just couldn't keep going if we didn't figure some things out first."

She chewed her lip as she looked at him. "What kind of things are those, Javier?"

"I know you're upset."

"I was in complete distress when you came to my rescue tonight. Of course I'm still a little distressed."

He pulled her to him with one arm, kissing her forehead. "You know that's not what I meant."

"Yes, I do know." She met his eyes. "But I thought that we were going to just enjoy ourselves and each other's company tonight, and leave it at that?"

"Can you leave it, though?"

She took another sip of coffee. "Yes."

He studied her a moment longer...she was quite certain that he didn't need all that much convincing to carry on as they were.

Then he surprised her by saying, "Do you think you could handle this long term?"

"Handle what?"

He reached up the sweatshirt, finding that she had no panties underneath it...she gasped as he felt her.

"Are you sore, yet?"

She exhaled. "I haven't had sex since the night before Bryson broke up with me."

"That's a record, isn't it?"

She nodded.

"Have I hurt you?"

She spread her legs as he continued to finger her. "I'm not sure which answer would satisfy you more."

"I never want to hurt you. Unless you want me to," he said.

"I'm sore, is all," she replied. "But you *did* say that you wanted me so sore that I can't sit down."

"I did."

She moaned softly as his fingers got a little too insistent, then she gently eased his hand away, closing her legs.

"If you want to talk about something serious, Javier, it's not fair if you distract me."

"I'm sorry."

"I just want to be with you. It's all that matters to me. But what did you have in mind?"

"Coming over regularly. Having me at your place."

"Are you talking about sleeping over, or do you want to be with me again? In a relationship?"

"No, Gloria. We both know that I'm wasting your time in a relationship, and that I want things that you can't give me."

She frowned, pulling away from him, wrapping her fingers around her mug. "Right."

"I didn't mean to hurt your feelings."

"You aren't hurting my feelings, you're being honest with me about your needs, and I appreciate that."

"Do you?"   She stood, walking to the other end of his porch. "I'd rather be hurt with the truth than to believe in false hope."

"It was a dumb idea. I know it would only hurt you...I'm a selfish prick sometimes, babygirl."

"We all are," Gloria said.

"So you don't want to just sleep together?"

She turned to face him again. "How can you 'just sleep together' with someone you have feelings for?"

"Very carefully."

"What happens when you get a girlfriend?"

"What happens when you get another boyfriend?" he countered.

She chewed her lip. "It won't work. It could never work."

He stood, closing the distance between them. "If you say so, babygirl."

She allowed him to take her into his arms. She wasn't sure what she wanted to happen next...she almost felt as though the mood had been broken, injected with too much reality. He wanted to discuss their future, but it certainly wasn't the future that she wanted.

"Javier," she said, after a few more moments, "I don't want to waste any more time."

"Okay, babygirl. Do you need more coffee?"

"No."

He took her hand and led her back into his house, to his bedroom.

For the rest of the night, they didn't talk about their future, or love, or how perfect they were for each other...they got in bed, he got inside her, and they didn't stop until neither one of them could handle any more.

The next morning, Gloria awoke with a pit in her stomach...though she was determined not to let Javier see or even sense it.

She gently sat up, being cautious not to rouse him as she grabbed for her phone on his dresser. How many nights had it been that way between them? That she'd woken up in his bed and grabbed for her phone, like she belonged there, with him?

She knew that she couldn't allow herself to fall into that way of thinking, so she checked her email and texts, seeing that both Bryson and Cynthia had text her. She ignored Bryson but confirmed her brunch with Cynthia, then she sat up, stretching.

Javier rolled over. "Is it already morning?"

"I'm afraid so," Gloria replied, with as much bravado as she could manage. She leaned over him and kissed him lightly. "I'm sure I have alcohol, vomit, and coffee breath."

"No, just coffee breath. And maybe cum."

She laughed. "Probably."

He wrapped his arms around her waist and drew her down on top of him; she'd thought he was going to start kissing her, but instead he simply held her, staring into her face.

"What are you doing?" she asked.

"Just...memorizing your beautiful face, babygirl."

She forced herself to smile. "I'm glad you think I'm beautiful."

"You *are*."

She leaned down to kiss him. "Javier...babe, I've got to go."

He sighed. "I was afraid of that."

She gave his lips another kiss...she was trying to memorize him, too...the way it felt to lie with him in his bed, the feel of his sheets against her bare skin...the feel of his body hair on her naked body, how safe she felt in his arms.

She knew that she would never find a man who felt so safe, who knew her so well and who could make her as happy as he made her.

She finally stood, easing out of his embrace. She smiled down at him and reached down to touch his face before she bent down to pick up her panties and bra off the floor, to get dressed to leave.

He watched her dress, then, as she eased her jumpsuit on, he got up and put on his clothes, too.

"Do you need anything to eat or drink before you go?"

"No," she said. "Cynthia and I are going to brunch. I guess I'll just go home and get ready to meet her."

He put his hand on her back. "Can you make it home?"

She nodded. "I'm much better than I was last night."

"I see that."

"I have you to thank for that."

He walked her to her car. His was parked on the street.

She turned to face him. "So...I had a good time last night. Thank you."

"No need to thank me," he said, softly.

"Well...I should leave, Javier."

He reached out to cup her cheek. "I know. I can't keep you."

Clearly, though, neither of them wanted her to leave.

She sighed, then wrapped her hand around the back of his neck and pulled him in. For one last kiss.

She kissed him desperately, with all of the possessiveness she wished she could claim over him, with all of her passion for him, the lust he'd reawakened and reignited within her...then, she forced herself to pull away.

She held his gaze a few more moments as he looked at her, breathless...she could tell that he was struggling, his head was spinning from her kiss.

She waited, hoping that she'd gotten through to him, that he'd realized how senseless it was that two people with such chemistry not be together.

But he smiled, sadly. "Too bad you don't want to be casual."

"Too bad you don't want to be exclusive."

"Baby, we *were* exclusive."

"If you say so." She sighed. "I love you. And I'll miss you...so fucking much."

He trailed his fingers over her cheek, across her jawline, and down her neck...one last time.

He looked at her wistfully. "I do love you."

"I know you do, Javier."

She finally made herself turn away, and to get into her car. It was the hardest thing she'd done since she'd left Henry, when she left Javier.

Because, as she backed her car out of his short driveway, she knew that was exactly what she was doing; she was leaving Javier.

Just like she'd said goodbye to her ex-husband the day before, that day, she knew, was the last time she'd see Javier.

She rolled down her window. "Thank you, Javier."

"Call me sometime. We could always just hang out."

She smiled, but she knew that she wouldn't do it. "Sure."

She gave him one last look, and—although all that she wanted to do was to put her car in park, get out, throw her arms around him, and never leave his side again—Gloria waved, rolled up her window, and drove toward her home.

3

CHAPTER THREE

Gloria parked her car in its spot, then got out on her shaking knees. She grabbed her handbag and tried to make it to her apartment before she broke down again...not as badly as she did the night before...before Javier had come to her rescue.

She tried to chalk her improved ability to deal with things to having had so much of her sexual tension relieved the night before...which almost made her believe that Javier was right, and that they *did* need each other for sex, and that they could still have somewhat of a relationship if fucking was all that the ever did together.

She walked into her apartment, tossing her handbag on her sofa as she walked to the kitchen for a glass of water...but she ended up pouring a glass of cranberry juice instead.

After all, she hadn't had sex in ages, and it didn't hurt to take some preemptive cautions.

She drank her juice, then carried her glass into her bedroom, sitting it on a coaster on her dresser as she shucked off yesterday's clothes. Once she got her jumpsuit off, she stood, staring at herself in the mirror over her dresser, taking in her appearance in her bra and panties...she knew she'd never wear them again.

Her heart wouldn't be able to take it.

She shucked those too, adding them to the pile in her floor before she drained the rest of her juice, then went to shower.

Gloria tried not to think about her shower the night before, as she allowed the hot water to envelop her, trying to wash away all that had happened...not because she didn't want to remember it, but because it hurt so goddamned much that she couldn't bear to.

She washed her hair, then grabbed the bar of soap and started scrubbing herself. God, it was hard to think about what had happened, and all that she had lost.

Just in that one night.

She washed between her legs, then she reached up inside her vagina and gently into her asshole, to make sure she got all of the cum out.

She heard her phone go off a couple of times, but she couldn't seem to get out of her shower. She kept it running, figuring that whoever it was could leave a message or text her.

Five minutes later, or so—it almost seemed as though time came to a standstill when she was in the shower...perhaps because it was the only time that Gloria really took out of her day to slow down, to only be doing one thing at a time, to focus only on the action at hand—she heard a loud knock at the bathroom door, followed by Cynthia shouting, "It's only me!"

She tried to steady her racing heart, now that she knew that someone hadn't broken into her house to murder her. "Oh, good! I would hate it if it were anyone else."

Cynthia laughed, coming into the bathroom. "I tried calling first."   "Yeah, I was in the shower."

"No kidding. So...how are you today?"

Well, as far as Cynthia knew, Gloria had just come home from her book signing and crashed, barely dragging herself out of the bed and into the shower in time to get ready for their brunch date.

She had no idea that Bryson had cornered Gloria in the parking lot after her signing, that he'd broken her—again—in the cruelest way imaginable...then that Gloria had spent the night with Javier, getting her brains fucked out and her mind fucked with, albeit of her own accord.

Gloria turned off the shower, and stepped out, grabbing a towel and wrapping herself in it. Cynthia took one look at Gloria's face, then she sat on the closed toilet seat. "Fuck."

Gloria leaned against her marble bathroom countertop, crossing her arms over her chest. "It's a bunch of bullshit."

"Let me guess...it has something to do with Bryson."

"And Javier," Gloria admitted.

"What the fuck are you doing, Gloria?"

"It's a long story. But...Bryson caught me in the parking lot after the signing."

"That fuckwad!"

"He wanted to take me for a coffee...but it was so late that I wanted to get a drink instead...so that I wouldn't be awake all night."

Which seemed stupid in retrospect, since she'd had copious amounts of coffee and sex the previous night.

"And? Damn it, Gloria, please tell me that you didn't sleep with him last night."

She laughed. "No, I spent the night with Javier."

"God, Gloria." She shook her head. "Why?"

"Because he came to get me from the bar."

Cynthia just stared at her.

"Bryson's got a girlfriend."

"Fuck."

"Oh, it gets better. She's..."

"What, Gloria?"

She swallowed hard. "She's having his baby..."

Cynthia stared at Gloria a few moments, like the news was sinking in. Then she stood up and walked over to Gloria, wrapping her arms around her.

"This isn't awkward or anything."

"We lived together for a year. I don't know how you get much closer than that."

Gloria laughed. "Like this."

"I'm glad you can laugh. I want to go find your scumbag ex-husband and kick his sorry ass."

"Doesn't matter. Javier came to my rescue."

"Yeah," Cynthia said, stepping back. "We're going to need to talk about that, too."

"I'll just get dressed..."

Gloria felt a tinge of fear creep into her stomach at the thought of leaving the house again...she'd barely made it home, although she'd promised Javier that she could make it. She'd been fueled by her desire to be home again, where she felt safe.

Where no one could leave her, assault her with bad news, or break her heart.

Cynthia put her hand on Gloria's shoulder. "It's okay...I think I'd rather order in and have it delivered."

"Really?"

Cynthia nodded. "I want to hear everything about your romantic evening with Javier."

"There's not a lot to tell...we fucked, and we agreed that we can't be together. I'm not planning to ever see him again, although he did offer to be friends with benefits."

"Oh, fuck," Cynthia said. "Fucker."

"Well...I don't think he's a fucker, necessarily. I love him. And he loves me. That's the problem. If it was like a situation with Alex, then it would be easy. Fuck him. But I love Javier."

"Well...are you going to keep sleeping with him?"

She looked at Cynthia. "You know I can't do that. I'll want more, and it will hurt us both."

"You're too goddamn mature, Gloria. You take what you want and demand more, or you're always going to end up missing out."

Gloria shook her head.

"Okay. Well, get dressed and I'll order us brunch."

Gloria went to her bedroom, dropping her towel and scooping it up, along with her jumpsuit, panties and bra.

She put them in different hampers, one for delicates and one for her regular laundry, then she went back to her dresser, choosing a t-shirt bra and cotton panties. She had no one to impress, although Gloria found slinky panties more comfortable than cotton. Thongs, however—no matter what anyone said—were terribly uncomfortable and really only meant for the pleasure of men, as was the majority of women's fashion. Any time Gloria went shopping—which was often, before she'd been in her latest depressive state—she tried her hardest to find real workout clothing, like shorts with bloomers in them, and tank tops that covered her boobs and belly, as the last place she ever tried to pick up a man was at the gym—when she was gross, sweaty and vulnerable—all she could find were sports bras meant to be worn as tops, skin-tight leggings (which were far too hot for hard workouts and running, as Gloria did), and crop tops.

Nothing she'd be caught dead in, if she could have found real, decent clothing with some modesty. As much of a total whore Gloria was in private, she liked to keep her public image modest and professional...just her personal preference. She knew how men were, talking shit about how women were such whores for simply living their lives and wearing makeup, trying to look good enough for those same men's entitled asses.

Gloria pulled on a soft green t-shirt and some terry cotton grey shorts, then she pulled on a pair of ankle socks, combed out her hair, and put some moisturizer on her face.

She debated filling in her brows...she'd had them micro-bladed, so old habits died hard, she supposed.

Gloria had used her money from being an author—once she'd been making enough money to pay all her bills comfortably, that is—she'd decided to have all of the cosmetic procedures done that she'd wanted to have all of her life. She'd wanted rhinoplasty since she was a teenager...she hadn't had it, though.

Henry had thought that she was beautiful. That had stuck with her for the past two years.

Gloria had never felt beautiful until Henry had told her that she was.

But she'd gotten her brows microbladed, gotten botox...she was thirty-two, after all, and for a woman, she may as well have been elderly.

And she had to keep herself up...she knew she was judged on her looks for her career, since she did public signings and events, and had social media. Also, she still—*desperately*—wanted to be married and to have a family. She couldn't attract a husband if she wasn't gorgeous and ageless.

Of course, Gloria had the money for cosmetic surgery when she was younger, living on the Alexander estate and living off of her family's fortune...but as a teenager, her mother had refused, and she hadn't had the guts to go for it while she'd still been living at home.

Then again, she hadn't met Henry yet, and he hadn't told her how beautiful she was. So maybe he wouldn't have thought she was as beautiful, if she had rhinoplasty or any other procedures done...if she'd had all of the moles on her body removed, to reveal a clean slate...but Henry had spent hours licking and biting her moles, worshipping every inch of her body.

Thank God she hadn't had those moles removed.

She finally made herself leave her bedroom—and those toxic fucking memories—to join her best friend in her open-concept living room/dining room/kitchen...basically the rest of her apartment aside from the two bedrooms, one her own bedroom, with the giant closet, the other her office.

Cynthia was sitting on the sofa, on her phone. Gloria pulled open the blinds, letting sunlight stream into her living room, then she sat on the opposite end of the sofa from Cynthia.

She'd figured that Cynthia was ordering food, but then she said, "I don't know, probably late afternoon. You can live without me that long, can't you?"

Cynthia clearly was speaking to Jordan. Gloria swallowed, curling her legs beneath her on the sofa. She tried to relax and make herself comfortable.

"Actually...that's not a bad idea. Uh-huh. Oh? Very sneaky." Cynthia laughed. "Fine. I'm not making any promises, though. Sure. I love you, baby. Bye."

She ended the call and tossed her phone aside on the sofa, then she turned to face Gloria, smiling.

Her smile seemed a little bit sneaky to Gloria. "Yes?"

"So, Jordan had a great idea. He's cooking dinner and wanted me to invite you."

"Jordan? Jordan is cooking dinner? He knows how to cook?"

Cynthia rolled her eyes. "You've got no room to talk."

"I suppose not."

"But yes, he's fixing Italian—which I know is your favorite—and you'd have a great time. I also don't think you should be alone after a night like you had last night."

"I'm fine," Gloria insisted.

"So you say, and it's fine. But please, come over tonight."

"Okay," Gloria agreed. "I'm starving. What did you order for brunch?"

"Brunch foods," Cynthia said, picking up Gloria's remote and turning on the tv.

"From where?"

"Mel's Drive-In. Ordered a ton of food, so you'd better be starving. Your skinny ass needs to eat."

"I was eating well before…"

"Well, it's not before, and you need to start eating again. I can't deal with you stopping eating every time you have a breakup."

"I'm sorry," Gloria said.

Cynthia sighed. "Okay, I know. I need to be more understanding."

"I just thought that I was done with this shit, you know? I truly believed I'd be with Bryson forever."

"Bryson is a dumb scumbag. Forget about him."

"He's really not, though. God, I can't believe he's already moved on."

"You know what that means then, don't you?"

Gloria felt her brow furrow as she looked at Cynthia, who seemed to know what she was talking about. "Are you about to say something that will upset me?"

"I wouldn't upset you—"

"Be honest."

Cynthia nodded. "I figured you'd rather that. Do you think he'd move on so quickly if he hadn't been…you know…"

"Cheating."

"Well." Cynthia nodded.

Gloria sighed. "I'm not perfect."

"What's that supposed to mean?"

"I've made mistakes, too. I dated Henry, after all. And Alex. Donovan…"

"Did you cheat on Bryson?"

"No."

"Really? You're sure about that?"

Gloria laughed. "Are you serious?"

She nodded.

"I might have. But only once I figured out that he was cheating on me." Gloria shrugged. "I wasn't going to divorce him over it. I decided to treat him the way that he was treating me."

"Who were you sleeping with?"

"I never slept with anyone. I was just…messaging this guy. It was nothing."

"So that's what Bryson was doing, too?"

"An actual sexual affair is so messy and risky. Like, what about STDs and pregnancy? But I'd be damned if I was going to divorce my husband, and I'd be even more damned if I let him have his online fling without having one of my own."

"This is so interesting. But, you're kind of famous. How did you keep this from coming out?"

"I'm not famous. Unless someone reads, they wouldn't know who I am at all."

"Oh."

"And I never sent him photos of my face, and I blurred all of my tattoos. I mean, he could tell I had a huge tattoo on my ass, of course, but there was no way to prove it was me, if he'd wanted to. I don't think he would have done that, though, anyway."

"You're too damn trusting for your own good."

"I guess I am, and apparently I'm never going to change, because I still wanted to pledge my love forever to Javier last night. I almost took him up on his offer, too…but I know that I'd start pressuring him for more, and I didn't want to do that to him."

"How noble," Cynthia said.

Gloria stared at her.

"Sorry, I know I'm being a bitch."

"It's okay."

"You deserve what you want."

"Even though I just admitted I was unfaithful to my husband?"

"He deserved it."

Gloria sighed. "Do you really believe that anyone deserves to have their trust broken that way? Even if they were doing the same, and they did it first?"

Cynthia stared at Gloria a few more moments, then she said, "Yes, I do."

Gloria shrugged as Cynthia switched to Netflix and started a show they'd watched together when they'd lived in Gloria's Hollywood apartment together, and they settled into a comfortable silence...the kind that only people who were that close and comfortable with each other could enjoy, as they watched their show and waited for their brunch to be delivered.

After the episode was almost over, Gloria's intercom went off and the person at her front desk let her know that her food had been delivered.

Gloria left Cynthia finishing the episode while she went downstairs to pick up the bags from the front desk.

"Smells good," the woman behind the desk said, as Gloria grabbed her bags.

She smiled. "My friend ordered brunch for us."

Gloria went back up to her apartment with the food.

Cynthia moved the placemats off of Gloria's glass-topped dining room table so that they could spread out their brunch containers.

Gloria brought their plates and silverware...she had all grey place settings that she'd gotten at a discount store, and she was insistent on all of her place settings matching, from the plates to the bowls to her mugs and glasses...Cynthia had teased her, that first Christmas they'd lived together, by buying her random cute mugs and glassware...which Gloria had left at her old apartment with Cynthia, when she'd moved out.

Then again, she hadn't really taken anything with her but her clothes when she'd moved in with Bryson, since he'd had a studio apartment.

"What would you like to drink?" Gloria asked, walking back to her kitchen and taking out a couple of frosted glasses from her freezer and adding her round ice cubes.

"Water is fine."

Gloria filled Cynthia's glass with water, then she filled her own glass halfway with water, and topped it off with more cranberry juice.

She went back to the dining room and set the glasses on the table before she went to her sofa-side table in her living room and grabbed some coasters she'd ordered online from someone's Big Cartel shop, because they were astrological coasters, and Gloria loved them...but she turned them upside down because she was afraid the condensation from the glasses may somehow mess them up.

Cynthia thought she was weird.

"Cranberry juice?"

Gloria sat down. "Yeah. Preemptive measure. I haven't had sex in months."

"Yeah. You must have gone hard."

Gloria laughed. "With Javier, it's always rough." She sighed. "And fucking amazing."

Cynthia nodded, taking the takeout containers out of their bags. "I got Avocado toast, fruit salad, and pancakes. I hope that sounds good to you."

Greasy food would have hit the spot...Gloria wasn't all that hungover, surprisingly... probably due to the coffee. Or, more than that, due to barfing up everything she'd had to drink in Javier's bathroom *before* the coffee...and before the shower sex.

God.

"Tell me," Cynthia said, serving herself pancakes and toast before passing the containers to Gloria, "what is it that's so great about getting fucked by Javier?"

"Really?"

"I'm dying to know. Does he beat you or some shit?"

"No!" Gloria said, taking out a pancake and two slices of toast. "He doesn't beat me, dumbass."

"Then tell me."

"He just knows what I like, and he always delivers."

"What do you like? What are you into these days, Gloria?"

"Why are you asking?"

"I'm curious. Was last night a good time or a bad one, because you're in a weird mood, and I can't really tell."

"It was good."

"Good."

"I wasn't ready for it to be over."

"What all did you do?"

"More like what *didn't* we do." Gloria shrugged. "He took care of me."

"I'm sure that you took care of him, too."

"He wasn't complaining," she replied, taking a bite of her toast.

"I bet he's missed you."

"We both miss each other. A lot."

"Right."

Gloria looked down at her pancakes. "It was more than the sex...although it was the best sex I've had in ages. He took care of me, made me coffee...talked to me the way that we used to talk, when we were together."

"You love him."

"Yeah. I do. I mean, I got over him...it took me forever, but I did." Gloria set down her fork and looked across the table at her friend. "When I was with Bryson, he was it. The only one, and I was prepared to remain devoted to that man for the rest of my life."

"Until he cheated."

"Shouldn't it be that way, though? You give a man the same back that he gives to you. I think it's only fair."

Cynthia stared at her friend for a long moment. "I suppose you really have changed a lot, Gloria. Two years ago, you gave your loyalty and love to complete trash."

"Yes."

"I like it."

"I loved Bryson."

"How did you find out he was cheating?"

Gloria laughed. "We lived in a studio apartment. I worked from home. It's not like it was that easy for him to hide anything. He couldn't stay up as late as me, so when he started being sneaky about texting, about taking his phone to the bathroom...I knew. Believe me, my past experiences made me quite intuitive to knowing when a man is doing sneaky shit."

"Did you confront him?"

"What was the point? He would have denied it. So, I took matters into my own hands. It was a lot easier for me to have an online affair than it was for him. I was at home all day, and I stayed up way later than he did, since he had to get up for work in the morning and I didn't." Gloria sighed. "Although he certainly used me to get himself off every morning. Fuck, I thought we were having sex, but he was using my body while he thought about *her*...and now she's fucking pregnant."

"That's a lot to deal with on your own."

"That's probably why I dealt with it poorly. I've got to be honest, though...I don't feel any remorse for what I did. I just hate that I used my body for revenge." She held Cynthia's gaze. "I don't care that I betrayed Bryson. He shouldn't have betrayed *me*."

"Does he know?"

"No, because he was too fucking focused on convincing himself—and me, but mostly himself—that I was in love with Javier. I suppose that made it easier for him to justify that he was cheating on me."

"That's sick, Gloria. I mean, I wouldn't blame you if you gave up on men."

"I wish I could." Gloria smiled, sadly. "But I need one too badly to give up on them."

They finished their brunch, washed dishes, cleaned the kitchen and dining room, then they went back to the sofa and their show, relaxing, not discussing affairs and the bullshit that was men again for that afternoon.

Around six, they started down toward the parking lot to go to Cynthia's house. Cynthia had gotten quieter, the closer it got to time to leave.

Finally, before they each got into their respective cars, she spoke up. "Gloria."

Gloria raised her eyebrows. "Yes?"

Cynthia exhaled. "There's something that I need to tell you."

"Okay?"

She hesitated. "It's not just going to be the three of us...Jordan invited one of his friends from work over for dinner, too."

Gloria shrugged. "Okay? I mean, that's fine?"

"But when I decided to invite you, too, I was thinking that it was maybe time for you to meet a new man..."

"Oh." Gloria rolled her eyes. "Of course."

"I'm sorry. If I would have known..."

"It's okay," she said. "It doesn't matter."

"Well, Jordan might have mentioned that you're single to this guy."

Gloria was about to get into her Taurus, but she hesitated, at that. "Did you invite him over, though, just so that I would meet him?" "I'm sorry. At the time, it seemed like a good idea."

Gloria forced herself to laugh, as genuinely as she could manage. "It's okay. It's a kind gesture. I'll be nice to him, but I can't guarantee that I'll want to go out with him."

"Just one date?"

"Cynthia."

"Please?"

Gloria shook her head, giving Cynthia a long look before she slid behind the wheel of her car and turned it on.

She didn't owe this guy a date...maybe if she hadn't had the experiences with her exes that she'd had the day before—night before—then she might have been horny enough to want to go out with him, might have even been tempted to have a one-night stand again...it hadn't happened since Alex, before Donovan.

But Javier had gotten the horniness out of her system and—other than feeling completely gutted from all that had happened, the heightened emotions—she was feeling more clear-headed than she had in months.

"Maybe."

Gloria was close to having an anxiety attack by the time she got to her old apartment with Cynthia. As soon as they headed up to the apartment, Cynthia could tell.

"Shit, I'm sorry, Gloria. I never should have done this—"

"You meant well. It's fine. Who knows. Maybe I'll like him. Or, maybe he won't like me. Plenty of men fall into that category."

"Only the stupid ones."

"You're going to have to be more specific than that. Too wide of a category."

Cynthia let them into the apartment...which smelled amazing. Gloria internally chastised herself for doubting Jordan's culinary skills...although perhaps she was getting ahead of herself. Maybe it only smelled good, but would taste terrible.

She wasn't quite sure why she was in such a negative mood.

She heard voices in the kitchen, so she followed Cynthia into the apartment, hanging her handbag and jacket over the back of a chair in the short foyer before joining everyone else in the apartment's small kitchen...it was a tight squeeze.

Jordan was stirring a pot of sauce, and his friend was sitting at the kitchen table.

He looked younger than Gloria. He was Indian, with brown skin and black hair. He was very handsome.

She swallowed, standing close to Cynthia, not sure why she was suddenly feeling shy.

Cynthia grabbed Gloria by her shoulders and yanked her around in front of her. "Noel, this is my best friend, Gloria Alexander."

Noel stood. He was about average height, maybe three or four inches taller than Gloria. He was dressed sharply, which she found incredibly attractive.

"It's very nice to meet you, Gloria."

She smiled, shaking his hand. "Nice meeting you."

He had on a dress shirt, and its sleeves were rolled up to his elbows...he'd likely been helping Jordan cook dinner. But, seeing his exposed arms, Gloria noted that he had a ton of dark hair on them...which made her knees weak.

Maybe Javier hadn't hammered all of the horniness out of Gloria, after all.

"I've heard a lot about you."

"Have you?" Gloria asked. "Interestingly enough, I've heard absolutely nothing about you."

"Why don't the two of you go make yourselves comfortable in the living room? Cynthia, I need your help setting the table," Jordan said.

Gloria—making sure that Noel couldn't see her—glared at Jordan's back, and gave Cynthia a *don't you dare* look.

Cynthia looked right at Gloria, smiling as she said, "That's a terrific idea!"

Gloria gave Cynthia a glare, then she turned to face Noel, smiling. "Okay, sure."

"Dinner will be ready soon."

"Right!"

She went into the living room with Noel, who sat on the sofa...she *did* at least manage to sit herself on the sofa cushion beside him.

"So...you work with Jordan?"

"Mechanical engineering."

"Jordan is a mechanic."

"I work on the engineering aspects."

"Interesting."

Noel laughed. "I know it's not the least bit interesting."

She smiled. At least he didn't take himself too seriously...or so it seemed.

"And you're a writer, I'm told?"

"Yes. Before I wrote, I worked in an office for nearly nine years, back in Atlanta." She hesitated. "Where are you from?"

"India, but I've lived all over Europe. Right now, I'm only here temporarily. I live in London."

Gloria nodded. "I used to live in England. Or, I lived in England for a few months, several years ago."

"That's what I was told. You didn't like it?"

"It was fine. I was engaged, and I left him."

"He wasn't good to you?"

She laughed, somewhat darkly. "No, he wasn't."

"Well, then I'm glad you left him. You seem like a nice girl. You shouldn't be with someone who doesn't treat you right."

She chewed her lip...hadn't Henry said that she was a nice girl, before he'd started fucking her? And look where that had gotten her...

"How do you know Cynthia?"

"She's my best friend. When I left England, I moved to L.A., and I looked for a roommate on Craigslist. Thankfully Cynthia applied and we hit it off. She's been my family. I owe her everything."

"And she works for you?"

"She's my assistant."

"Then you must really be famous."

It made Gloria a little nervous, that she was talking to another Englishman...even if he was from India, he lived in England, and she couldn't help wondering if he was going to end up being just like Henry? Were all Englishmen cut from the same shitty cloth?

Or was it just all men, in general?

"I wouldn't say I'm a household name or anything. Not most households, anyway." She smiled.

"Well, you must do pretty well though, being a full-time author."

"I could be doing worse." She hesitated, wondering if she should say something to break the ice when it came to her writing career and the nature of that which she wrote. "Do you know what kind of books I write?"

"Jordan says you're a romance writer."

Gloria decided in that moment that she hated Jordan for putting her in that situation. If he expected her to go out with that guy, he at least should have given him a warning.

She smiled, grimly. "I wouldn't quite put it that way."

"Oh?"

Gloria sighed. "I write erotica."

"Oh." He laughed, somewhat awkwardly. "Okay. Interesting."

She wanted to die. "I take it that when *you* say that, you really mean it. Or, you're looking for a nice way of saying that you're not exactly thrilled about it?"

Noel shrugged. "Why wouldn't I be, though? You write fiction."

She nodded. "That, I do."

"Well...I see nothing wrong with that."

"Good."

Although, she wasn't quite sure why she'd called it good...it didn't really matter to her one way or another what he thought of her.

She longed for dinner to be ready so that she wouldn't have to keep up that uncomfortable conversation...if she wouldn't have feared it being rude, she would have gotten up right then and gone home, no explanation given to Cynthia or to fucking Jordan.

But she didn't want Noel to think that he was the reason why she left...even though he would have been a part of it.

"So, Jordan did mention that you're recently divorced."

She flinched inwardly. "Well, it's been several months."

"I'm sorry. That couldn't have been easy."

She met his eyes. "Have you ever been married, Noel?"

"No. I've really only had two girlfriends."

Oh, fuck, Gloria thought...not another one, a man who was useless in bed like her ex before Henry. In all honesty, Gloria would have taken ten men like Henry over one man like her ex. She would rather be treated badly than to be bored.

"Oh. Um...when did you last date?"

"I had my old girlfriend in my early twenties, from twenty-three to twenty-five. Then I dated my most recent ex when I was twenty-seven."

"Oh. Did you love them?"

She wasn't sure at all why she'd asked. She figured that she apparently just wanted to make things more awkward.

"Eh, no? My first girlfriend was more of a relationship of convenience. My other ex cheated on me."

"I'm sorry," Gloria said.

"It's fine." He shrugged.

"I wasn't fine when my ex cheated on me."

"Your ex-husband?"

Gloria shrugged...she supposed it wouldn't really have been fair to air out that particular piece of dirty laundry about Bryson. He had been respectful toward her during their divorce, even when she'd made things difficult for him.

Not that she didn't feel as though he'd deserved it.

"Sorry, too personal."

"If you really wanted to get personal, you should know something." She held his gaze. "It's important to me to make sure anyone I meet knows this about me before we take things any further."

"What's that?" Noel asked.

"I'm a submissive. And I take my role very seriously."

He nodded. "Okay. So, that means…"

"I have specific sexual preferences, and I need those preferences to be fulfilled."

"Alright."

She smiled. "That's it. That's what I needed you to know."

"I don't know a lot about BDSM."

"I don't blame you. Most people who know about it on a casual level don't understand what it's really about, and it means something different to every person who practices it."

"Sounds complicated."

"I've had guys turn me down because I was asking too much, wanting a BDSM dynamic in a relationship. Because it *is* a lot of work."

"Do you only date…?"

"Dominants." Gloria nodded. "Usually. Although, many of them don't want the same things that I want."

"Which is?"

"I want marriage and a family."

She felt as though she had nothing to lose. She wasn't afraid to put it all out there, to say exactly what it was that she was looking for in a relationship…she was already thirty-two, and she really didn't have any time to waste when it came to finding someone to settle down with.

And her desperation and longing was—of course—amplified by the fact that she had been recently divorced from the man who she had believed would be the one to give her everything.

"So do I," Noel said. "How many children do you want?"

"I say that I want two, so that they will always have each other," Gloria said, "but if I'm being greedy—and honest—I want four."

He nodded. "Well, I'm glad to know that you'd like to have children."

"How many would you like?" Gloria asked.

"Well, I'm Catholic, but my sister only has one daughter. I know it's traditional for Catholics to have large families."

"So, you want a large family, or no?"

"I don't really know."

"But are you ready for children now?" she asked. "By the way, how old are you?"

"I'm thirty. And, I'm planning to move back to London in a few weeks."

Gloria nodded. "So I suppose that it doesn't matter, these questions I'm asking you?"

"Well, you used to live in England."

"For a few months, and I've been in Los Angeles for two years now. It's my home now, more than Atlanta ever was, even."

"But would you move back to England, Gloria?"

For Henry, she thought...and she was alarmed by her thought. She rarely even *thought* of Henry; the only reason she had said his name in bed with Javier was because Javier was the first man to fuck her so good from behind since she'd been with Henry...it had been an honest mistake.

"I don't think so, I'm happy here in Los Angeles."

Noel looked at her for a long moment, nodding. "Okay."

She thought it odd that he'd asked her that question...he seemed like a serious man, but to have not even been on a date yet and to already be asking if she'd relocate for him. Then again, he hadn't really asked her that. He'd asked her if she'd ever live in England again. And she'd asked him how many children he wanted.

Perhaps their craziness was evident of their need to be together?

"I'm thirty-two," Gloria said.

"You're young."

She laughed. "Older than you."

"What is it that you want in life, Gloria? Is it to be a famous author, or to be a mother and a wife?"

"Why couldn't I be both?"

"You absolutely can. I was only asking which you want the most."

"I'm already as famous of an author as I'd like to be. So, I guess I'd have to say the wife and mother part is what calls to me the most, right now."

"Are you in a hurry?"

"I'm thirty-two. Women don't really get to wait until they feel ready, like men do."

"That's true. It's not really fair, is it?"

She shrugged. "It's life."

Then Jordan stepped out of the kitchen. "Dinner is ready."

Noel stood, then held out his hand to help Gloria to her feet. She hadn't been expecting that, but she took his hand and allowed him to help her.

He didn't let go of her hand as he led her into the kitchen, and Gloria didn't protest ...although the smug look on Jordan's face pissed her off thoroughly.

Noel pulled her chair out for her...she'd only been into the overly chivalrous act with Henry and with Bryson, but perhaps that was because Alex, Donovan, and Javier hadn't pulled it—although it was sincere for some—so she hadn't minded its absence.

Based off what she knew of Noel, from the twenty or so minutes she'd known him suggested that the gentlemanly act came natural to him.

A part of her wondered if that should have been a red flag...

Cynthia took her seat across from her, and Jordan sat across from Noel.

She swallowed. "Do you pray before you eat, Noel?"

"I don't want to make anyone uncomfortable..."

"You won't. Don't worry about it." She glanced over at him.

He nodded, then bowed his head. "Bless us, O Lord, and these, Thy gifts, which we are about to receive from Thy bounty. Through Christ, our Lord. Amen." Then he crossed himself.

Jordan nodded. "Um. Thank you, Noel. So...dig in and please don't tell me that you hate it."

The spaghetti dinner was wonderful, made with homemade marinara sauce, although the pasta was store-bought. He'd cut up and prepared a Greek salad, too, which was wonderful. Along with thick-sliced garlic bread, the dinner was wonderful, and so was the conversation...Gloria was aware of her reaction to Noel, of how she kept her eyes on him as much as she could, of how she kept the conversation going between them.

She knew that Jordan and Cynthia were aware, too...she caught the sneaky, self-satisfied glances they kept stealing at each other.

Bastards.

But Gloria was also grateful...having a new person to date—if it came to that—was an excellent way to cope with her experience the night before, with losing Javier and finding out her recently ex-husband had already knocked another woman up.

After, they cleared the table—or, Jordan and Cynthia cleared the table, while they sent Noel and Gloria to the living room to continue their conversation.

"What does the rest of your week look like?" Noel asked, smiling at her.

She smiled. "I'm an author. I make my own hours, so the rest of my week looks however I want it to look."

"Would you like to have dinner Friday evening?"

"I would love that."

"Where would you like to go? You're the person who lives here, you know all the good restaurants."

"Well, would you like to go somewhere fancy, or more casual?"

"You look like a woman who deserves fine dining."

She laughed. "No man has ever said that to me."

"Well, they should have."

"Have you ever been to The Stinking Rose?"

"Once, when I first came here."

"Would you like to meet me there?"

"I would...but I would feel much better if you let me pick you up."

She wondered if it should have concerned her, having him know where she lived...but if things went well, then he would end up at her apartment, anyway.

"Okay. That's very considerate of you."

"You deserve to be treated like a queen."

Hadn't Henry spoken those exact words to her? But she liked Noel...he was handsome, he was stylish, he was charming...she wanted to get to know him better, and she couldn't really get to know him at all if she couldn't seem to shut down her worried mind.

Thank all of her toxic relationships for that...but she also refused to allow her past to keep her from giving her heart to someone else who might end up being her future.

She ignored that cautioning voice in the back of her head warning her that she was getting ahead of herself. She wanted to be fucking happy.

She thought that, after all the shit she'd been through, she deserved some happiness. If Noel was the one that her happiness could be found with, that made it all that much better.

Jordan and Cynthia rejoined them, then. They brought coffee and dessert, which was biscotti...Gloria's favorite Italian dessert. She wasn't a fan of coffee, of course, but Cynthia knew that and had more so made Gloria's milk with some coffee splashed into it...which—to Gloria—complimented the biscotti beautifully.

Not as beautifully as Noel seemed to compliment her and everything she'd ever wanted in a man...

Maybe not everything, ever. There had been a time—before Henry—when Gloria had truly believed that what she wanted in a man was a partner, someone who would be faithful to her and who would love her, who would be gentle and kind to her.

Then she'd had the complete opposite in Henry, and he was the first man she'd ever loved, and he'd made her crave the exact opposite of everything she'd thought that she wanted.

And since she'd been married to Bryson, he'd been such a different man...as dominant as they came, but fair and worthy. He'd been respectful and he'd genuinely cared about her and her feelings...until he hadn't, she supposed, when he'd decided that it was easier to cheat on her than it was to try to fix whatever it was that he felt was lacking in their relationship.

Perhaps, she figured, since Noel had been cheated on, he would be more sensitive to her fears and doubts, because he'd been there, too. He could relate.

Also, she was naive enough to believe that he would never cheat on her, knowing the pain of having had his trust betrayed.

She glanced over at him, suddenly wanting to tell him everything, to share all of her pain with him.

She wanted to let him in...fuck having her guard up. She still had a heart to love with, and she wanted it so desperately in return.

She wondered if Noel couldn't be the one to give that to her.

She was willing to bet that he was. Maybe it was desperation, maybe she was still far too much of a romantic, but either way, she had no intention of throwing it away before she could see how far it might go.

And she was ready to give it a shot to see what would come of it. Not to mention that Noel was hot and she did want to sleep with him...but she'd let him take her to dinner first.

Just to make sure.

"You like Italian, then?" Noel asked, watching Gloria eat her biscotti.

"She buys biscotti at the store and eats it for breakfast some days," Cynthia said.

"Are you Italian?"

Gloria shook her head. "My mother's family is from Great Britain and my father's family is from Scotland."

"Do you enjoy English or Scottish food, then?"

She wrinkled her nose. "Well, I've never had anything Scottish, but my ex ate beans and toast every day, and I hated it."

He laughed. "I've maybe had it twice in my life. I'm not a fan, either. Do you enjoy cooking?"

Cynthia laughed.

Gloria rolled her eyes. "I can cook oatmeal, and microwave dinners, and that's about the extent of my culinary skills, I'm afraid. My husband did all of the cooking, when we were married. He tried teaching me, but he gave up after the third or fourth meal I burned."

"That's fine," Noel said.

"Do you enjoy cooking?"

"I do. I don't have much of a choice, if I want to eat."

"What do you like to cook?"

While they were in the midst of their conversation, Gloria was vaguely aware of Cynthia and Jordan leaving the living room and stepping out onto the tiny balcony just outside the second-floor apartment.

"All kinds of things. I enjoy trying new recipes."

"That's impressive to someone who can't even bake a potato," Gloria said.

"I'm sure you're good at lots of other things," Noel said.

She wanted to show him what she was good at...so she decided to try liasoning their conversation from earlier back to the present.

"Does it bother you, Noel, that I'm older than you?"

"No," he said. "Does it bother you that I'm younger than you?"

"I only dated one guy who was younger than me...he was twenty-eight when I was thirty. So, the same age gap as between the two of us."

"How did the relationship go?"

She chewed her lip. "Well, it wasn't much of a relationship. We were only sleeping with each other."

"Do you normally have casual relationships like that one, Gloria?"

"You mean sexual relationships?"

He nodded.

"He was the only one. I don't enjoy casual flings, Noel. Especially not those of a sexual nature. It's not safe physically, of course—without taking extra cautions—but it's also unsafe for me mentally and emotionally."

"I agree. As I said, I've only had two sexual partners in my life. Both have been my girlfriends at the time."

"I didn't set out to have a casual fling. I thought...well, I didn't believe that he loved me, but I thought that we were going to be together for a while."

"Did you love *him*?" Noel asked.

"No...I don't think so. I'd just gotten out of my relationship with my ex—the English one—and he gave me attention. I was hurting a lot, and I was lonely. I needed someone, and he was there. I just thought...I thought that he'd enjoy the sex and that he'd agree to be my dominant, but he said that it was too much responsibility."

"I'm sorry, Gloria."

She shrugged, pretending to be unaffected...it had been a long time, really, since she'd thought much about Alex and what an asshole he had been. He was just one more man on the long list of exes Gloria had, who she'd given too much to, who hadn't wanted to give as much as she'd wanted from them.

She looked at him again. "So...how old were you when you lost your virginity?"

He raised his eyebrows, and Gloria briefly wondered if she'd crossed a line too quickly.

"I was twenty-three. With my girlfriend."

"Did you love her?"

"I may have thought so, at one time, but I know better now. We weren't compatible." Gloria nodded.

"And you?"

"Are you asking me how old I was when I lost my virginity?"

"Yes."

He almost seemed embarrassed, like he worried he'd offended her by asking her the same question she had asked him.

Not remotely.

"I was eighteen," she lied.

"Did you love him?"

Gloria laughed. "As a friend. I just wanted to lose my virginity to him, and I knew it for a long time before I finally convinced him."

"But you weren't in love?"

"No."

Just then, Cynthia and Jordan returned from the balcony. Cynthia was crying, but she looked happy. So did Jordan

Cynthia held up her left hand, showing Gloria. "I'm engaged!"

Gloria got up off the sofa and went to hug her friend. "I'm so happy for you," she said.

Cynthia pulled back, a huge smile on her face as she looked at Gloria. "Thank you."

Noel stood, moving to shake Jordan's hand. "Congratulations."

"I'm glad that the two of you are here for this," Jordan said.

Gloria wasn't sure why that was, but she supposed it didn't matter. Cynthia and Jordan's engagement mattered, and the last thing she wanted was to do or say anything to take away from that moment for them.

The rest of the evening was spent celebrating Cynthia and Jordan, and their engagement. They had a celebratory drink...beers for the men, wine for the women, when Cynthia pulled Gloria out onto the balcony to talk in private.

"Were you expecting this?" Gloria asked, lifting her wine glass to her lips for a long sip.

"Not entirely. I knew that he was up to something...but then I thought it was because he wanted to fix you up with Noel. That was sneaky, using that to distract me."

"Would you have rather been alone with him—I mean, without company—than to have us here?"

Cynthia smiled. "Once you two leave, we'll have plenty of alone time. And, believe me, I intend to make the most of that alone time."

Gloria smiled back. "Good for you."

"Are you upset?"

"About your engagement?" she asked, frowning.

"No, about Noel."

Gloria looked down, her face feeling hot. "No, I think I like Noel."

Cynthia grabbed her arm. "That's amazing! God, I'm happy."

"He's really...well, frankly, he's hot."

"Isn't he?" Cynthia laughed. "Okay, I don't feel guilty anymore."

"You shouldn't feel guilty. I know everything you do, you do it out of the goodness of your heart, and out of genuine concern for me." Gloria hesitated. "But what you need to do now is to focus on your engagement. When do you think that the wedding will be?"

"I don't know...I'm not like you, Gloria. I don't want to elope. I've always wanted a big fancy wedding." She sighed. "I know how lame and ridiculous that is."

Gloria didn't think that it was lame *or* ridiculous...having grown up as a debutante, she'd been to her share of huge, elaborate weddings, and she'd known that was what her mother and father had expected for her, too...until things had changed.

"You get to have whatever kind of wedding you want. And, truth be told, most women *don't* want to elope, Cynthia."

She smiled. "Okay. Um...will you help me, though?"

"Of course I'll help you."

"Good."

They went back inside, and Gloria announced that she needed to be getting home, knowing that Cynthia and Jordan wanted to be alone to celebrate their engagement together.

Noel took the hint. "I'll be leaving too. I'm very happy for you both."

Gloria hugged Cynthia again. "I'm very happy for you."

"Thank you. I'll call you tomorrow."

"Alright."

"I'll walk you to your car, Gloria," Noel offered.

"What a gentleman," Cynthia said, smiling at them both.

When Noel's back was turned, Gloria rolled her eyes pointedly at Cynthia, then followed Noel out of the apartment and down the stairs to her car.

"Which car is yours?"

"The black Taurus."

"It's a lovely car."

"Thank you. I bought it before the divorce, but my apartment is from divorce money."

He looked at her like he wasn't sure if she was being serious or joking.

She smiled. "It was nice of you to walk me out here."

"It's no problem at all."

She nodded. "Well, it was nice meeting you, Noel. I'm looking forward to Friday night."

Even as she spoke the words, she sort of wondered if she was being too forward. Like if saying 'Friday night' instead of just 'Friday' implied anything.

Then again, she wanted to be honest. She really did hope that he wanted to sleep together Friday night, but—considering how few women he'd slept with—she wasn't sure that he'd want to.

Which was fine.

She told herself.

"So am I." He hesitated, looking at her...not the way that Javier had looked at her, but in a way that made her feel nice. Maybe it didn't make her feel like tossing him her panties, but it was still nice. "Gloria...may I kiss you?"

She smiled. "Of course."

He stepped closer, and he put his hand underneath her chin, lifting her face to his. He leaned in, and she closed her eyes as he softly brushed his lips against hers.

His lips were so warm and soft. His kiss was gentle, tender even. It didn't make her want to press her body against his and take her clothes off, but perhaps that was because that wasn't what he was trying to achieve though that particular kiss.

Didn't mean that he wouldn't at a later date. At least him kissing her showed his interest...so she wanted her kiss in return to show her intent. She reached up to wrap her arms around him, gently stroking his back as she returned his kiss. She eased her lips slightly open, inviting him, and she felt his tongue brush—very gently—against her lower lip.

She gave a soft moan, then eased away, ending their kiss. She wanted to leave him wanting more.

Before she showed him how she'd give him everything.

He lightly trailed his fingers over her jawline, looking into her eyes. "Drive home safely, Gloria."

"I will. Let me give you my number."

He took out his phone, and she gave her number, then she opened her car door, lightly tossing her handbag into her passenger seat.

"I'll call you," he said. "And I'll meet you at your place on Friday night. Around seven? And I'll make reservations for seven-thirty."

"I'll send you my address."

He leaned in and kissed her forehead. "Have a nice night, Gloria."

She smiled at him, then she got into her car.

Gloria went to bed that night, exhausted but happy. She was happy for Cynthia, and she was excited about her date Friday night. She was eager to get to know Noel better. She desperately wanted another relationship; if she were perfectly honest with herself, though, she knew that she wanted to replicate her relationship with Bryson. She wanted to be married again, wanted to have one man to sleep with for the rest of her life...a man who would be faithful, and to whom she would give her loyalty in return.

Because she wanted a happy marriage and a family. She'd thought that she'd had a happy marriage with Bryson. But then, apparently she had been the only one to be happy with it.

Part of her regretted not confronting him about his affair, but the other part of her had known that she'd done him wrong, too...not because she'd wanted to, but because she'd felt she *had* to do so, in order to get even, in a way. She truly hated to look at it that way, but—based on what she'd experienced in the past, with Henry, Alex, Donovan, and even Javier—she knew that honesty on her part could be twisted to manipulate her into fitting whatever narrative was convenient for whomever she was sleeping with at the time.

But if she'd not been so vindictive, if she'd played the fucking victim about his affair, maybe he would have felt guilty enough to go to counseling and to save their marriage...although Gloria also knew that men like him were always going to go back to cheating.

Bryson might end up cheating on his new girlfriend...maybe not, since she was pregnant with his baby.

If only Gloria had gotten pregnant before he'd divorced her.

If only she'd had Henry's baby...

She was startled by that line of thinking, toxic as it was. The last thing that she needed to be doing, as she started off a new relationship, was to be thinking about *Henry*, of all fucking people.

She decided to just wash her face and go to bed when she got home...she was exhausted from the night before.

She also had a lot to think about.

She took off her clothes and went to her bathroom, grabbing her jar of makeup remover to begin her skincare routine for the night...it was so nice to be almost too exhausted from her day and night before to do her skincare routine, than the usual reason why she was too tired...from simply being drained by her depression.

She didn't want to think about those weeks that had turned into months, after Bryson had left her...although it was hard *not* to remember them. Perhaps she didn't remember the specific details, but she recalled the pain and emptiness of getting into her bed every night alone, cold to the bone, so lonely and heartbroken that she'd truly believed that her chest might cave in.

That she would die alone.

But she wasn't so hopeless that night. She told herself that, even if things didn't work out with Noel, she had Javier, and that—if she got lonely enough—she could call him and at least she wouldn't sleep alone for a night.

That was what she had hated so much, the nighttime. Of course, the mornings hadn't been much better, waking up alone to an empty apartment. She hadn't thought she'd ever have to experience being alone, when she'd married Bryson. Truthfully Gloria never *had* been alone. She had lived with family, then Henry, then she had lived with Cynthia...then she'd moved into Bryson's apartment.

Then again, it concerned her, the idea of getting involved with a man who was planning to move back to London. She was prepared to give her soul and her body, but she knew the soul-crushing, bone-crushing pain of losing someone she loved with her whole heart. Then again, she supposed that she was getting ahead of herself in thinking that she was going to fall in love with Noel.

But she didn't want a meaningless sexual affair. She wanted a deep connection with the next person she slept with.

There was a strong part of Gloria that wanted to make a vow to herself...one that she wouldn't break easily. A vow in which she promised herself that she wouldn't have sex with another man until they were engaged, at the very least, if not married...she highly doubted that she would find a man willing to date her and to love her enough to marry her *without* getting to fuck her first, but she could hold out the hope.

In an ideal world, she would have insisted that her future husband wait until they were engaged before she would sleep with him...it almost seemed manipulative on her part, but as long as her boyfriend understood where she was coming from...

She wasn't naive enough to believe that any man was that understanding.

But Noel might be, she couldn't help thinking.

Two days later, Gloria was getting ready for her date with Noel. She had worked out that morning. She'd been eating much better since the night she'd gone over to Cynthia's...she wanted to believe that she was doing better on her own accord, because she had pulled it together and had decided that she was going to start being better to herself, and to start living her life again, and that she was going to learn how to do it without Bryson.

But she worried that her newfound mental health was due to the possibility of romance that she had with Noel. She had thought about him a lot over the few days since she'd seen him. It had been such a long time since Gloria had dated someone who wasn't a dominant. She wondered if she could be satisfied with a vanilla relationship...how it would feel to have sex without the pressures of performing as a submissive...if she'd enjoy it or not.

She was very nervous, admittingly. She felt like there was a lot at stake with Noel; she wasn't sure how she would cope if things didn't work out between the two of them. She knew that meant that she was completely dependent upon the attention and affection of a man, but she'd already knew that.

At the same time, she couldn't help thinking that, after all she'd been through emotionally in romantic relationships, she deserved something to finally work out for her.

She deserved true, lasting love.

She'd showered thoroughly, exfoliating and shaving absolutely everything. It wasn't as though Gloria had skimped on being ready for intimacy...which was all the more reason why she'd had zero reluctance to jump into bed with Javier, unplanned. She was also still on birth control, even though she'd been close to stopping them when she had still been with Bryson.

She suddenly realized, as she was sitting in front of her vanity mirror in her closet, that Bryson had ended their marriage just before she was supposed to finish her last pack of pills...it was like he'd been waiting until the last moment to tear the rug out from under her, to destroy her life, to snatch away everything that she loved...had he been waiting until the last moment because he was heartbroken at the idea of leaving her, or...?

She knew that if she dwelled on it too much, she would fall apart and be a wreck before her date, so she did all that she could to bury those feelings. Instead, she began doing her makeup. She began with her Tacha moisturizer, smoothing it over her skin...she *had* continued to get her cosmetic treatments since her divorce, and it had made her feel *incredible*—albeit momentarily—to spend her ex-husband's money on stretch-mark treatment, a chemical peel, and even a vaginal rejuvenation. She'd felt it only fair, to cleanse her vaginal canal of eighteen-months of her ex-husband.

So, as she did her makeup for her date that night, she noticed how easily her moisturizer and primer went on, her skin was so smooth and crease-free from high-end, routine skincare and expensive treatments.

She did her eyebrows...which only required brushing through them with gel, since she'd had them microbladed. Then she carved them out with her Nars concealer, smoothing it out with her mini makeup sponge. Next she did her eyeshadow, using a small Nars palette that Bryson had given her for her birthday that year. She then did her contour—still necessary, unlike her eyebrows, since she hadn't had rhinoplasty—and put her Teinte Idole foundation to blend out her cream contour.

Then she took her Nars concealer under her eyes and on the sides and middle of her nose, blended those out with her sponge, then set her concealer with her Hourglass setting veil. She took her powder contour on top of that, then she did her bronzer and blush. She touched up her brows with some brown eyeshadow, brushed them out again, touched up her eyeshadow, then lined her water line in a nude pencil, and lined her eyes with her liquid liner.

She finished off her makeup look with her Benefit mascara and her highlighter, then set it all with her setting spray. When she got ready, she always started out with her outfit, then she did her makeup, then she did her hair. She finished off with perfume and jewelry.

That evening getting ready was no different. She got up from her makeup chair and stood in front of her mirror, making sure that she hadn't gotten any makeup on her black sleeveless dress that was cut to her decolletage and to just the tops of her breasts, if she bent over or pulled her dress hemline down a little bit.

The dress was tight to her waist, then slightly looser and more flowy at its bottom, which fell to her mid-thighs. She'd worn pantyhose underneath, since the dress was so short. She wasn't wearing a bra since it was low-cut, but she had on a silky nude colored thong underneath her pantyhose, and she was planning on carrying a small YSL black clutch that—again—had been a gift from Bryson, and matching black YSL heels.

She saw no chance that she'd be wearing any new designer anything, since Bryson was the one who had spoiled her, and—although she made enough money to live comfortably—she didn't have nearly enough money to go shopping very often. But, Gloria could have her procedures, she could buy her fresh foods and could afford to eat healthy, and she could pay her utility bills, car payment, insurance, streaming services, fuel for her gas-guzzling car...all off of her writing royalties, so in her mind, she was doing incredibly well financially, even if she didn't have a BMW or a new Prada bag every month, and if she only went shopping at Beverly Center a couple of times a year.

That wasn't to say that she didn't sometimes miss her weekly shopping trips, having new clothes whenever she wanted...but she missed having Bryson far more than she missed his money.

That all-too-familiar sharp pain shot through her chest, the emptiness threatening to cave in on her as she thought about how she wasn't going through the motions of getting ready to go out to dinner with her husband, for a special date-night dinner after he got home from work.

They wouldn't be spending a sexy evening teasing each other delectably, yet subtly, throughout dinner, only to come home to his cozy, immaculate studio apartment and fucking each other senseless, late into the evening...she wouldn't have that safe familiarity that she'd had with Bryson.

Another reason she wanted things to work out with Noel was because she wasn't sure how many more times she had it in her to give her heart, body, and soul away to someone new.

She wanted to fall in love one more time...and she wanted it to be for life, with a man who would give her a family, and would give her his loyalty and love in return for her complete devotion.

And she hoped that she'd found that in Noel—when they'd not even been on a proper date, at that, yet—and that it was the last time she'd have to get to know someone new.

She went to her bathroom to do her hair. She'd washed it and let it air dry, where it had dried into its soft little waves. She sprayed it down—not too much, so that Noel could run his fingers through it, if he liked, later—but enough to where her waves would hold their shape without getting fuzzy.

Back in her closet, she applied her YSL Black Opium perfume, then put on a gold necklace and matching chunky gold chain around her left wrist.

She was so nervous.

She stepped into her shoes, grabbed her bag, and made sure she had everything she needed...her wallet, lipstick, a tampon and panty-liner, just in case.

She still needed her phone.

Back in her bedroom, Gloria grabbed her phone off her dresser and checked it for messages...she had a text from Cynthia, wishing her luck.

She was texting her back a "Thanks!" when the person at the front desk buzzed her to let her know that someone was there for her.

She checked her reflection one last time in the mirror over the table in her foyer, then she locked her apartment up and went down the elevator to the ground floor, where Noel was waiting for her.

He looked so nice, wearing a suit. When she went in to hug him, she smelled his cologne...he smelled exquisite. It wasn't anything like Bryson had worn, but reminded her of the cologne that her friends with benefits when she'd been a freshman in college had worn.

She'd always loved that cologne. Smelling it brought back good memories.

He pulled back from their embrace, then took her hand in his. "You look beautiful."

"You look nice, too."

She smiled.

"Well, I guess we should be going, if we have reservations."

He walked her out of her building, to a Toyota Corolla parked in one of the fifteen-minute spots at the entrance of her complex.

"It's just a rental. And could I tell you how difficult it is to adjust to driving on the opposite side of the road? Not to mention having a car that has its steering wheel on the wrong side."

"It's only the wrong side in England," she said, smiling at him.

"Did it bother you whilst you were living in England?"

"My boyfriend didn't really drive much. He didn't have a car. Didn't need one."

"I don't drive in London, either. Where did he live?"

"Blackpool."

"Oh, right."

"It was so pretty there, and I liked that it was close to the ocean. I love the ocean. Although, sadly, as close as I live to the Pacific, I don't visit the beach often."

"When you visit, which do you like to go to?"

"Santa Monica or Venice."

"Very nice areas."

"Much nicer than the place my ex lived in Blackpool." She shrugged. "He didn't want me going out alone because he didn't feel his neighborhood was safe. Although...I've lived on my own in Los Angeles for two years and I went to college in Atlanta, so I don't think that was it. I mean, sure, it was a new country, but I more so think that he wanted another way to control me."

They stopped by his car. She stood at the passenger door, and he moved like he was going to open her door for her...then, when she'd said what she said about her ex not letting her leave the house on her own—about him controlling her—he hesitated, leaning in closer to her.

She smelled his cologne again...it was intoxicating, but perhaps not as intoxicating as his very presence.

"He controlled you?"

She nodded. "He was my dominant."

"Was he...did he abuse you?"

She swallowed.

"I'm sorry. That was too personal."

"No. It's not too personal. Um...yeah, he was. Emotionally more than physically..."

"Did he ever hit you?"

She took a deep breath. "Not...not unless I wanted him to."

He stared at her a few more moments, and she wondered if he thought she was crazy, if he feared that being with her would be too much, if she was the embodiment of a red flag...but Gloria was going to fully be herself, and she meant to be completely honest with him, about absolutely everything.

So, if her true-self was too much for him, at least she'd let him know exactly what he was getting with her.

But Noel reached out and gently cupped her chin in his hand, making her slightly close her eyes, fighting the moan that wanted to come from her throat.

She felt his breath on her face.

He leaned in and pressed his lips gently against hers...she wasn't sure if he only meant it to be a soft, quick kiss, but her whole body reacted to him. She instinctively reached up and wrapped her arms around him, her hand against the back of his neck, guiding his face down to hers, closer, as she pressed her body against his. She opened her mouth as he kissed her...she should have waited to see what he would do, how he would react to her slightly-parted lips, but her hormones wouldn't allow her to be patient and soft with him. She eased her tongue into his mouth.

She felt him slightly tense, and she rubbed the back of his neck as she reached her other hand up to press against his chest. His tension must have simply come from surprise, because he reacted quickly, holding her closer, his hand against her back, his hand—still under her chin—moving gently against her, as he caressed her chin with his thumb.

She loved how he touched her, and she ached to feel more of his touch, wondering how his hand would feel on other parts of her body.

As he touched his tongue more confidently to hers, she moaned into his mouth, and she felt his lips turn upward into a smile, against hers. She pulled him a little closer, wanting to feel his tender kiss a little longer, prolonging it as much as she could, without overwhelming him.

She need not have worried, as they gently parted, but he still held her in his arms, looking down at her.

Her heart twisted in her chest, and she smiled up at him, sighing.

He smiled. "You're a very good kisser, Gloria."

"So are you."

He leaned down to kiss her forehead, hugging her tightly for a moment, before he gently released her, opening her car door.

She got in, and he closed her door, going around to get into the driver's side.

When he closed his door and started the car, he looked over at her. "You're also very beautiful, Gloria."

"Thank you."

"Sometimes I still can't believe that you wanted to date me. When Jordan showed me a photo of you, I thought he was mad to think that you'd be interested in me. You're not shallow at all."

She laughed. "You're very handsome."

"Oh, Gloria, flattery will get you everywhere."

"I'll keep that in mind."

He pulled out of her complex and onto the road. Gloria flipped down his mirror visor and reapplied her lipstick.

"I guess I messed up your makeup."

"Don't worry, Noel. I have eight-million lipsticks."

"Do you?"

"Of course. Which color do you like best?"

Henry had wanted her to always keep her nails red, and he liked red lipstick on her. He was her only dominant who had wanted her nails to be a specific color. Even Bryson hadn't minded, although she'd learned—through all the men she'd dated—that men liked painted nails, so she had kept hers manicured since learning that.

Of course, she hadn't painted her nails red since she'd been with Henry. She couldn't bring herself to do so.

"Oh, I have no idea. I haven't thought a lot about different shades of lipstick."

"Well, if you think of a color you like, let me know. I'll wear it on our next date."

"I like whatever you like...but I definitely like the idea of us having another date."

"I'm glad."

They had a lovely dinner at The Stinking Rose. Gloria was a little worried that Noel was spending too much money on their meal; he'd already paid the valet, although she'd offered to cover it.

When she'd gone out with Bryson, of course, she'd never thought twice about the bill. He was her husband and they shared a bank account, for one thing, but, more than that, Bryson was *quite* wealthy.

She knew that Noel had a good job, but she highly doubted that he made anywhere near what Bryson made...and surely he didn't make as much as Gloria and Bryson combined had made...which made Gloria a little sad.

It wasn't at all that the money mattered so much to her, but the thought of being a part of something, like she'd been in her marriage to Bryson...she missed it terribly.

He had ordered lavishly for them at the restaurant, whatever he made. Gloria assumed that Noel had an idea of how much the bill would be, that he would have looked up the menu beforehand. He'd also said that he had eaten there once, when he first moved to L.A.

He'd ordered them Bagna Calda, first off...along with their garlic potato soup as an appetiser, which made Gloria happy, because it was her favorite thing to eat at The Stinking Rose. She was delighted that he ordered shrimp pasta, because Gloria liked their pasta and pizza best there, too. She ordered the garlic noodles, which—after the soup—was another of her favorites.

He ordered them a bottle of wine...it was going to be a *huge* ticket.

She hoped that he could afford it, that he wasn't bankrupting himself for her. She didn't want to not enjoy their evening together because she was worried about his money.

She smiled, spreading some garlic on her bread. "I love this restaurant."

"Do you eat here a lot?"

"Well...I did come here about once or twice a month with my ex-husband." She chewed her bread, wondering how bad it was for her to be discussing what she did with her ex-husband with the guy she was seeing and trying to impress.

Then again, she *was* trying to be authentic with him...

"Right. Gloria, I'm sorry. I'm sure that was very painful for you."

She took a sip of her wine. "That's an understatement."

"You must have really been in love with him."

"Of course I was. He was my husband, you know?"

She *refused* to cry on their first date—it wasn't as though she'd not done enough, already, to potentially dissuade him—so she tried to pull it together.

"I don't mean to upset you."

"Noel, I've got to stop allowing it to affect me. *He's* moved on."

"Do you mind me asking what happened?"

"Do you mean, whose fault it was?"

"No, not necessarily."

She chewed her lip.

"Did he...was he...?"

"Unfaithful?"

"I was going to say 'abusive.'"

"Oh, no. Absolutely not...he was very, very good to me. We were so happy...or, *I* was happy. I thought that Bryson was happy, too. We were about to..."

Gloria couldn't finish. She clenched her jaw, then her hands together in her lap, wondering if she could tell him, and feeling as though she absolutely *had to* tell him...

Gloria took another sip of her wine.

"Are you okay?"

"It's hard to talk about."

"Then we don't have to discuss it, darling."

Her heart gave a little skip when he called her that. Gloria was such a sucker for pet names that it was almost embarrassing.

It was almost as though a man could call her 'babe,' and she was his...she knew she had issues with that, but she'd done nothing to remedy that, save acknowledging it.

"I can tell you've been through a lot. I'm sorry."

"We've all been through a lot," she said, shrugging as she took a spoonful of her soup. "I'm not special. I've made a lot of bad decisions when it comes to men."

"But he was your husband."

"Marriage is complicated. Whether or not it should be. I thought it was simple: you love someone enough to want to spend the rest of your life with that one person. They're the only other person you'll ever sleep with, and you acknowledge and admit to that when you take your vows."

"Apparently to some, Noel, vows don't mean anything."

"But they should. A marriage should be sacred."

Gloria knew better than to fall for words, but it was hard *not* to, when a man seemed to know exactly what she wanted to hear.

And it always turned her on way more than it should have.

"I agree. And I took my vows seriously. Until I found out that he hadn't done the same. Up until the end...I never knew it was the end. He caught me off-guard, and it was very difficult for me to learn how to live without him."

Their pasta dishes were delivered. Gloria realized she was talking *way* too much about her ex-husband, and that Noel had said very little about his own life.

"I've been talking way too much. I want to know about your life. Where all have you lived? Where are you from initially?"

The remainder of the dinner was far more enjoyable to Gloria, as she listened to Noel talking about his life. He'd been born in India, and he'd gone to London for school, and gotten a degree in mechanical engineering. He'd worked in Sweden for a while, then in Italy, before he'd settled in London.

"I got the opportunity to take a temporary position in Los Angeles, so I took it. I'd always wanted to travel to the U.S."

"Do you like it?"

"It's a lot like London in some ways...except I can't take the bus everywhere and it's sunny and the weather is nice. We don't see a lot of sun in London."

"Will you miss it when you return home?" she asked.

"I'll miss you, Gloria, I'm afraid."

She felt a painful twist in her gut, which made no sense, considering she'd just met him...but she also felt that—despite the fact she knew better, she'd learned better over her many heartbreaks—she was already beginning to fall for him, and to envision a future with the two of them being together.

"Well, don't miss me. Stay here in Los Angeles."

"It's a little crazy, isn't it? Already thinking about altering my future for a girl I just met?"

"Not as crazy, Noel, as me thinking about changing *my* future, if you don't change yours." She shrugged. "I love L.A., but my lease is almost up. I only signed for three months. When the divorce was final, I moved into my apartment on impulse...I was doing a lot of impulsive things at that time." Not that she still wasn't. "And I moved to England to be with my ex the first time I met him. He came to see me, and I couldn't bear the thought of him leaving me."

"Are you telling me that you want to move back to London with me?"

"I moved with Henry because I was in love."

"How did you know you were in love, the first time you met him?"

She held his gaze. "Sometimes, you just know."

He drove her home after their meal, which had cost $130, but Gloria hadn't wanted to insult him by offering to help with the bill. She assumed he figured that she was accustomed to luxury and the finer things in life—which she admittingly was—but love was the luxury that Gloria craved most.

On the drive home, Noel reached over for her hand. She sighed at the feel of his fingers between hers. His touch was so soft and gentle and completely alien to her.

It made her heart hammer in her chest, made her ache between her legs...because if he touched her hands that gently, she could only imagine how gentle everything else would be...how his fingers would feel against her skin...on her nipples...

...inside her.

They kept up their easy conversation, but the closer they got to her complex, the more she could sense his unease and his nerves. A part of her was wary, wondering how much sexual prowess he truly possessed...if he'd only had two sexual partners in his life, maybe he hadn't had enough experience to know, really, how it was done. The last thing Gloria needed was to relive the god-awful sex she'd had with her boyfriend she'd had before she'd met Henry...he had fumbled his way inside her clumsily, which always hurt—not in a good, intentional way—and he'd thrust clumsily in her a few times, sloppily kissing her or groping her roughly before she'd felt him cum inside her. And he'd always fallen asleep immediately after, like the effort of it had been too much. There had never been any cuddling or kissing after—not that Gloria had really felt up to giving that man any affection, after feeling so used and *never* getting off, with him—and the closest he ever got to it was falling asleep right on top of her, still, with his heavy weight crushing her chest.

She'd always tried to shove him off of her, but he'd been too heavy, and he'd been snoring away and was impossible to wake, so she had always had to crawl out from underneath him, gasping for breath when she'd finally freed herself of the burden of him, gathering as much of the blankets and sheets and pillow as she could and retreating to her side of the bed, grateful she had a California King that still gave her ample room to sleep, even with her ex-boyfriend's massive bulk right in its center.

She'd always been so irritated, too, when she'd have to wiggle out from under him, and he'd fall out of her and get semen all over her sheets. Every fucking time he'd slept over at her place, she'd had to change her sheets the moment he finally left.

Then Henry, thankfully—for as much damage as he'd done—had come after, had made her work for it, had finally understood that sex wasn't something to be given dutifully, just because you were dating and it was expected, but that it was something to be earned...and it had gone both ways.

Of course, Henry had hardly had to exert any effort to turn her on and to make her needy and willing enough to do everything he asked, but *she* had certainly had to work for it, for every touch, every kiss, every kind word, *and* every orgasm, as denying her had been his favorite activity.

She wanted someone who was somewhere in the middle—but closer to the scale of Henry than of her ex-boyfriend—but if she had to choose, she'd rather have someone like Henry.

But Gloria's ex hadn't even been a good kisser, and Noel had already proven that he was skilled at that particular act. She'd decided, after she'd broken up with her ex for the third and final time, that any man she dated henceforth, she would kiss on the first date, and if he wasn't any good, then it would be the last date.

But, then again, she'd met Henry, and she'd become as she was, desperate and willing to do anything for affection and attention.

God, she hoped that Noel was the one, because she wasn't sure how many more first dates and getting to know someone she had in her. She'd thought she was done, when she'd married Bryson...but leave it to a man to change his mind, to go back on the promises he'd made to her, and to ruin her life.

If she weren't so goddamned addicted to men, she would never have dated again.

But she was, and she would.

Noel pulled up in front of her apartment complex.

She'd already made her mind, so she turned to him. "I had a really nice time."

"So did I, Gloria," he said, cupping her cheek in his hand and brushing her hair back with his other hand.

He leaned in to kiss her, as she'd known he would, and they kissed like they had at the beginning of their date, mouths open, tongues active.

She moaned as she leaned closer, pressing as much of her body against his as she could.

He reached down to cup her back, then his arms went around her waist as she reached up, holding his face to hers.

She arched her back, pressing her breasts up against him, wishing desperately that he would reach down to gently fondle them, to cup them so that she could feel his touch as he worshipped her body.

She moaned, deepening the kiss, giving him every signal that she could think of, short of taking his hand and putting it on her breast.

Finally, he worked his hand up her back, and she pulled back, kissing his neck, still letting out little moans, encouraging him to make his move.

He finally touched her neck, looking briefly down into her eyes, before she went back to stroking his chest and kissing his neck, breathing in the spicy scent of his cologne.

He worked his hand down her neck, over her collarbone, making her gasp. She closed her eyes, working her hands to the buttons of his shirt and undoing a few, so that she could ease her fingers inside his shirt and stroke his chest...she ached between her legs when she felt how hairy he was. She needed to feel his hairy chest against her bare flesh.

She craved him.

He finally ran his fingertips along her cleavage, which barely showed over the line of her dress. Again, she arched against him, and he took the hint, cupping her left breast in his hand, through her dress, and he eased his fingers beneath the line of her dress on her right breast, working his fingers against the gentle swell of her breast, as he fingered her erect nipple on her left side.

She worked her hands slowly down his chest, reaching down, lightly brushing her fingers over the bulge in his trousers.

He wanted her...or, his body did, at least.

She put her hands back on his face, looking briefly into his eyes before she leaned in to kiss him, but she'd seen the burning desire and lust in his eyes, and she knew that she was doing all of the right things.

"Noel," she whispered, her lips against his.

"What, darling?"

"Do you want to come up to my apartment?"

He looked down, holding her cheek in his hand. His left hand was still on her breast, teasing her nipple through her dress.

She chewed her lip, waiting for his response. She'd thought that he'd given her all the signals to let her know it was what he wanted.

She hoped she wasn't being too forward. But, if he thought she was a whore…well, she kind of was one.

"I don't want you to feel pressured."

She smiled. "You're sweet. I don't want *you* to feel pressured."

"I'm just not used to women inviting me up to their rooms on the first date."

"I'm sorry—"

"No," he said, "I would like to come up with you."

She leaned in and kissed his cheek. "Good."

She buttoned his shirt back, and she kissed him again as she readjusted her dress. He got out and came around to help her out of his car, then she took his hand as they headed back into her apartment, heading to the elevator.

"These are nice flats."

She smiled. "Do you have roommates back in London?"

"No, I only have one here because I'm here temporarily and am still paying on my flat in London. But I live alone. My flat is tiny."

She nodded, leaning against him as they waited for the elevator to reach her floor. "My ex had a small house. One bedroom, a living room/kitchen combination, and the bathroom. My apartment is pretty much the same, but it's got two bedrooms and it's a little larger. I also have a washer/dryer and dishwasher."

"Very fancy."

She shrugged. "It's nice…honestly it's a lot nicer than my ex-husband's apartment. But that was kind of why I got it. I thought it would make me feel empowered, but it just makes me lonely, because it means there's that much more emptiness."

He wrapped his arm around her shoulders. "I'm sorry."

He kissed the top of her head, and the doors opened to her floor. She took his hand and led him down the hallway, outside her apartment, where she keyed in the code and let him inside.

"Welcome," she said. "Make yourself at home."

"You could fit five of my flat into yours," he said.

She shrugged. "My ex-husband had a studio, which is one room. I was happier there than I am here…although, it *is* nice to have the extra bedroom and closet. I admittingly have a lot of clothes, but I use the guest room as my office, too."

She had the feeling that he was still as horny then as he'd been while they were making out in his rental car, but she also felt as though she needed to slow things down a little...more so for his sake than for hers.

She really liked him, and she wanted him...but she didn't want to scare him off.

But her hormones were synapsing ridiculously fast and furiously. She desperately wanted to take him to her bed, and she wanted to find out everything that the two of them could do with each other.

"This is the living room/dining room/kitchen. Paying three-thousand dollars a month for an apartment in West Hollywood gets you basically three rooms, not including your bathrooms."

"Three-thousand pounds in London doesn't get you half of this."

She smiled at him. "And you're trying to get me to move there with you?"

He reached out to twist his fingers through her hair. "It's worth a try, isn't it?"

"Come see the rest of my apartment, Noel."

She opened the door on the left-hand side of the hallway. "This is my guest room and my office. I had my office set up in the living room of my old apartment, and I wrote from the kitchen table, or our bed, in the apartment I shared with my ex-husband."

The room was smaller than her bedroom, which, in itself, wasn't very large, either. The guest room held a twin bed, a dresser, and a nightstand, and had flowy curtains over the floor-length windows across from the bed, where she had her desk setup. On her desk was a file organizer with all of her notebooks and planners, a cup holding pencils and pens, her printer, and her new MacBook Pro, which didn't have a cracked screen.

As soon as Bryson had seen that she'd been writing on a busted laptop—which still worked properly, however—he'd immediately gone to the mall and purchased her a new one...although this one was much nicer than the one she'd had when she'd left her home in Atlanta. She'd written on a MacBook Air, with minimal storage and which she only used for word processing and formatting her books.

Bryson had bought her a Behemoth of a MacBook Pro, with all of the extra storage, the strongest processor available, and all of the extra software available, as well...even though all she'd asked for was Microsoft Word. Gloria never used her new laptop for more than writing and formatting, though.

Sometimes she wanted to sell that laptop and get her something simple...something that didn't remind her of her ex-husband every time she opened its lid to write.

She turned to face Noel, forcing thoughts of Bryson away. "This is where I do all my work, such as it is."

"It's bigger than my bedroom in my flat."

She smiled. "Want to see where I sleep?"

She waited for him to take her bait, having asked him in as neutral of a position as she could have had him in...not asking him while she was kissing him, or as she started undressing.

"I do."

She saw that same darkness in his eyes that she'd seen in his car, when she'd been kissing him and touching him. She longed to reach out and touch him again, right there...but she made herself hold back, to exercise some restraint.

She did, however, take his hand again as she guided him across the hallway to her bedroom, the master suite of her apartment.

Her own bedroom was considerably larger than the guest room. Her king bed took up most of the room, but she had a dresser, and a nightstand on either side of her bed. The same floor-to-ceiling windows were covered with the same curtains as she had in her guest room.

She turned on the floor lamp beside her bed, then she sat. "Come in. Like I said before, make yourself comfortable, Noel."

She leaned back, watching him, watching his dark eyes grow even darker as he took her in, as he familiarized himself with her bedroom...

"It's okay," she told him.

He approached her, stopping just in front of her, at the foot of her bed, where she sat. Gloria strategically opened her legs a little bit...wondering if he could smell her dampness, as she'd felt it seeping into her panties from when he'd been stroking her nipple in his car. Again, she arched her back, easing her chest forward, holding his gaze.

"It's okay," she repeated, lowering her voice and speaking more softly. "If you want it, Noel, it's yours."

He was breathing heavily as he knelt in front of her. He leaned in between her slightly spread thighs—as spread as her dress would allow—and he placed a hand on either of her knees. She smiled down at him, moving her hips toward the end of the bed, encouraging him.

He slowly eased her skirt up her thighs, his fingers brushing the nylon of her tights...she could still feel the heat of his touch through the skin-tight material. He looked into her eyes as he leaned in and pressed his mouth against her inner-thigh.

As prepared as Gloria thought that she was for him...she'd been sorely wrong. She shuddered at the feel of his mouth against her sensitive flesh...even with her hose in the way.

She gasped. "Noel."

"I think we need to get rid of these," he told her, reaching up underneath the rest of the skirt of her dress.

Her eyes rolled back in her head, and she moaned as his fingers brushed against the waist of her hose. He tugged them out from her thong, easing them down her thighs with grace that surprised her...hosiery was a tricky item of clothing to remove.

He eased her hose off, along with her heels, kissing the inside of the arch of her foot. ..fuck, she'd never known that her foot's arch could be an erogenous area...just...*fuck*.

He slowly worked his way up her body, kissing the inside of her ankles, her calves...t hen, he was kissing her inner-thighs, and without the thin material of her hose between their flesh, she shuddered and whimpered as he worked his way closer and closer to where she wanted him to be.

Without moving her skirt up too high and revealing all of her body to him, he eased his hand on up, his fingers brushing against her thong, the slick—and wet—material between her legs. She gasped as he eased his finger underneath the fabric...still looking into her eyes as his fingertip softly brushed against the lips of her labia.

"Oh. Noel."

"Keep saying my name like that, baby."

She whimpered as he eased her folds apart and slipped his left index finger inside her, finding her dripping wet and ready for him to take her. But he moved slowly, rubbing his finger all along her insides as she lied back across the mattress, her legs spread wide, her skirt still over her upper-thighs.

She felt herself instinctively beginning to push back against him as he finger-fucked her...and the movement of her hips became more insistent and desperate, the deeper he probed her.

"Please," she finally panted, feeling herself start to foam with all of his thrusting and probing...she was close, painfully close, but every time she was almost there, he pulled out a little, eased back on the intensity.

In response to her pleas, he pulled his fingers out and moved his body over hers...for the first time since he'd started his fucking magic on her, she realized that he was still fully dressed, and she wasn't okay with it.

"You need to take your clothes off, Noel."

He leaned in and briefly kissed her mouth, pulling back to give her a look of triumph. "I want you to undress me, my love."

She moaned as she wrapped herself around him...both her arms and her legs, as she tugged him closer, so that he was lying on top of her. Even then, as forceful as he was being, she noticed him still shifting his weight over her, so that she wasn't carrying the whole burden of his bulk...not that he was terribly bulky.

He was in excellent shape.

She rolled him over so that they were on their sides, facing each other. She held his gaze for a brief moment, then she began unbuttoning his shirt again, easing it off his shoulders, reveling in his bare skin, brown and covered in dark hair. She reached out, rubbing her fingers over it...god, he was fucking exquisite. A masterpiece.

Instinctively, she reached out and held him against her with her face pressed against his skin and her arms around his waist. She kissed him, working her mouth across his chest, down his stomach as she stroked up and down his biceps and triceps. She couldn't get enough of him, proven as she kissed and tasted and stroked him...down to his belt.

She sat up, urging him onto his back as she straddled him, her hands on the buckle of his leather belt.

She heard his heavy breathing as she unbuckled his belt, unbuttoned his fly, then tugged down his zipper. She tugged his pants down his hips, and he lifted them to aid her in undressing him.

She heard him moan as she moved back up his body, easing her fingers inside his briefs.

She felt how hard he was, so she wasted no more time in teasing him...with as hard as he was breathing, she wasn't sure how much longer he would last.

She removed his underwear...then *she* was the one who was fully dressed.

She moaned. "I didn't know you're not circumcised."

"Is that a problem?"

She cupped him in her hands as she looked up into his eyes. "Not at all."

She started working her hands over him, then she took him into her mouth, feeling him twitching against her lips and the roof of her mouth.

He reached down and twisted his fingers through her hair. "Gloria."

"What's wrong?'

He stroked the back of her neck as she looked at him. "It's more comfortable for me to wear a condom when I'm getting head."

"Okay," she said, sitting back.

"Do I need to get one?"

"I have some. Just give me a minute."

She stroked his chest and moved back up his body, kissing his lips before she got out of bed and went to her bathroom.

She never used condoms, but she kept some in supply, just in case. She hadn't planned on ever having sex with a random stranger—again—but, being a complete whore, she had a sex toy arsenal, and condoms were included in her collection.

Sometimes Henry had wanted her to use unconventional items as dildos, so she always sheathed those items before she'd use them inside her.

She had some flavored condoms, so she grabbed a couple—and a few regular ones, and some lube, since he wanted a condom—and she went back to bed.

He had his hand on his dick.

"Not getting started without me, are you?" she asked, straddling him again.

"Just keeping him warm."

She laughed, then she ripped open one of the flavored condoms and slipped it over him, looking into his eyes as she moved down over him, and took him in her mouth.

She'd been curious as to how it would feel to suck an uncircumcised cock, but she supposed she'd have to find that out on another day.

She sucked him off...loving how his hips came off the bed as he thrust shallowly into her mouth. He was so much more gentle than any other man she'd gone down on.

And he definitely knew what he was doing.

He didn't finish inside her mouth, though. He pulled out of her mouth. "You need to take that dress off."

She smiled, moving her hair to one side as she moved up the bed, her back to him so that he could unzip her dress.

He moved the straps off her shoulders, her dress falling to her waist. He cupped her breasts as he shifted his weight; Gloria turned to face him.

He looked at her. "Gloria, you're a remarkable woman."

She smiled as his mouth descended upon hers.

He kissed her tenderly, easing her back on the bed, completely removing her dress as she lied before him in her thong.

He kissed his way down her body, her breasts, sucking her nipples, making her back arch off the bed. Then he worked his way down her belly, to the line of her underwear.

He eased her panties down her hips. She lifted her knees and spread her legs as he put his face between her thighs, tasting her.

God, he was exquisite. She shuddered as he lapped at her, as his tongue entered her, then as he circled her clit. She moaned, trembling.

He stuck a finger inside her, then another, swirling them around gently. He removed his fingers, feeling how wet and ready she was.

"Are you on birth control?" he asked.

She nodded.

He ripped off the condom and he moved back up her body, keeping one hand between their legs. He cupped the back of her neck with his other hand, then he kissed her as his fingers circled her clit, as she whimpered and opened her mouth, welcoming him inside her in more than one place.

He moved his other hand to his penis, and he guided himself inside her.

She relaxed her muscles to allow him inside her, shifting her hips, moving down to him as he entered her. She moaned, loving how smooth and soft his skin felt, marveling at how much better it felt with silky skin easing the blunt head inside her.

He wrapped his other arm around her hips, holding her body tightly to his as he began moving his hips, thrusting and twisting as he kissed her.

She held onto his shoulder and his back, matching his thrusts with her own, throwing her head back...sex hadn't felt that good in a long time.

Not even from the other night, with Javier.

He knew just how to position himself as he took her, in the way that felt best, like he was an expert on female anatomy. She lost herself in the thrusts, in her little whimpers and moans as he nearly made her come, then he'd ease up, like he knew exactly where she was, how close.

And that he wasn't ready for her to succumb to her impending orgasm, yet.

Then he pulled out, making her whimper in protest.

"Flip over."

She smiled, turning over smoothly, getting onto her hands and knees, arching her back and spreading her legs as she positioned herself to take him.

He grabbed onto her hips and thrust inside her from that different angle, hitting her perfectly so that she nearly orgasmed from his penetration alone.

He was more relentless that time, clearly ready to come, too. He thrust faster and harder, making her gasp, making that tingle rise up her back, as the stretch burned inside her.

"How do you like this hard brown cock, baby?"

She whimpered. "Fuck. I love it, Noel."

He grabbed a handful of her hair. "How much do you like it?"

She began pushing back against him. "Fuck."

"Good."

He slapped her butt, hard, making her gasp, bringing her even closer.   "Noel, I'm about to come."

"Not yet."

He kept pulling her hair.

"Choke me," she said.

If her request caught him off-guard, he didn't show it. He simply moved his hand from her hair to her neck, keeping his hold light...which was fine, since he likely didn't know how to choke a woman properly.

But having a hand around her throat was enough for Gloria, as she felt herself getting close.

"I'm coming," Noel said.

"Yes."

"Fuck," he said, holding her against him by her hips as he pounded deep and hard inside her.

She felt his hot cum shooting inside her. A lot of it. She tightened her muscles around him, grinding her hips against him so that he hit her in just the right spot, making her begin to throb and clench around him.

As she came, she kept feeling him shooting more and more semen inside her. He removed his hand from her neck as he took her hips by both hands, shoving deeper inside her, so much that she ached, that the sensation was too much. She started moaning in pain, as her body jerked against him.

He gave her butt one more hard slap before he released his hold on her, letting his penis fall out of her. "Fuck, Gloria."

She was feeling it, too. Her legs were shaking so hard that she couldn't hold herself up any longer, so she lied on her back, reaching for him.

He lowered his body beside hers, wrapping his arms around her.

If Gloria was crazy, that was fine. It wouldn't be the first time, but she knew—without a doubt—what she wanted, and what she had to do to make it happen.

She reached up to take his face in her hands. "Noel."

He reached down to stroke her cheek. "What is it, darling?"

"When you move back to London...I want you to take me with you."

4

—·—

CHAPTER FOUR

G loria had been back in England for three weeks.

In that amount of time, she'd managed to get moved, get settled into Noel's tiny flat with him, and get everything back in Los Angeles sorted out, as well.

Not that any of those things had been that important to her...neither had her writing, for that matter. At least, not for her first week in London. She'd been far too consumed by her need for Noel, as she'd not been able to get enough of him...and there had been times that she hadn't thought she would ever be able to let him leave the bed.

Their bed, at that point. In his London flat—which was, as he'd told her back in L.A., tiny—he had a full-size bed, which took up most of his bedroom. She'd settled right in. Her bed back in L.A. had been far more comfortable, of course...but she'd slept in it alone, which she'd hated.

In fact, living in Noel's tiny flat with him reminded her so much of living in Bryson's one-bedroom apartment, when she'd been her happiest.

After she'd told him to take her back to London with him—after Gloria had fucked him only once—Noel had instantly agreed. If he'd thought her insane, he hadn't said so...she knew he was a much more practical person than she was, but he'd wanted her with him. She liked to believe that theirs was a whirlwind romance, and that they were destined for each other...that they were in love...although, deep down, Gloria knew better.

But she loved England, and—despite the fact that she also loved Los Angeles—she felt like she belonged there, more than she did in the U.S. So, even if she wasn't in love and didn't marry Noel and have his babies—which was her plan—at least she lived in the right place.

And she refused to think about Henry.

She'd not renewed her L.A. lease, but she'd rented out a large storage unit, which didn't cost all that much less than her first apartment in Hollywood. She'd had her furniture moved there, her paintings, some of her clothing. She hadn't brought a lot with her to England, since there wasn't a ton of room for two people in Noel's London flat.

But she'd brought enough, and Noel's flat was crowded. Of course, the most important thing that Gloria had brought with her had been her laptop, which she'd been using a lot more often since Noel had gone back to work at the beginning of that second week there in London.

The first few days, he'd stayed with her, showing her around and helping her get settled. And, of course, they'd spent a lot of time in bed together, seemingly *still* unable to get enough of each other's company.

Among other things, other reasons.

After that first time they'd had sex, Gloria hadn't wanted to allow him to leave her apartment, let alone her bed. He *had* ended up staying with her throughout the remainder of his time there in Los Angeles, and Gloria—along with help from Cynthia—had arranged everything for Gloria's expat to London.

"I'm really going to miss you," Cynthia had said, hugging her at the airport when she and Jordan dropped Noel and Gloria off to catch their flight to New York, where they'd get on another plane for London.

"I'll miss you," Gloria said, feeling her heart stammer at the thought of leaving her friend, the one person who had been with her through everything since she'd first come to Los Angeles, broken and alone, two years earlier.

"It sucks that you won't be here to help with the wedding planning."

"I can still help you, booking things online and such. We can text and video chat all the time."

Cynthia nodded. "No, you're right. Besides, it was my and Jordan's idea to introduce you and Noel. We should have known this would happen."

Gloria had also had a hard time—though she never would have admitted it—leaving Los Angeles for the other people she was leaving behind...namely, Javier.

And Bryson.

Then again, Bryson was done and over with, but Javier had given her the option of continuing a sexual relationship...which she likely would have taken him up on, had she not met Noel.

Things had been amazing when she and Noel had been holed up in her bedroom in Los Angeles...celebrating their love—if it *was* love—and fucking each other numb.

He was an incredible lover, bringing her to heights she'd never known...not even with Henry, who had depended upon emotional manipulation and the raw intensity to get her off.

Noel was intricate, complicated in all of the best ways. She'd been addicted, unable to do or to even think of anything else...even when they'd made it to London, and she had so much resettling to do, Gloria had been unable to think of much else than being in his bed, making it *their* bed...getting off intensely, every time.

Then he'd gone back to work, and she had started writing again...and he'd inspired her anew, giving her a whole arsenal of experiences to write about, adding authenticity to her erotic novels.

That night, it was later than usual when Gloria heard Noel returning home. She'd been caught up in her story, and catching up on all of the writing she *hadn't* been doing since she'd met and fallen for Noel.

But she'd gotten a lot done that day, and she wanted to reward herself by indulging in her lover, to whom she was already connected and committed.

She shut the lid of her laptop and slid it underneath her side of their bed, then she got up and left the bedroom to greet him.

He was taking off his shoes and putting down his bag when she reached him.

"Hi," she said, wrapping a hand around the back of his neck when he turned to face her.

He smiled. "Hello, darling."

He kissed her...but there was no real warmth to his kiss, which seemed more perfunctory than anything else.

She noticed that he carried a takeout bag in his hand. "Did you pick up dinner?"

"I picked up dinner for you...I was invited for drinks at the pub this evening."

She felt a strange pressure on her chest. "Okay."

"I didn't think I'd have time to fix you dinner before I go, so I brought you some takeaway, soup and salad."

She smiled, but it felt empty. "Thank you."

"I wanted to let you know I'll be home late. Don't want you to worry about me."

"Sure."

He reached around her to place the takeout bag on the kitchen counter, then he touched her cheek. "Are you okay, darling?"

"I missed you today."

"Oh. Well...I'll see you when I get home."

She chewed her lip. "Okay."

"Aww, Gloria, I'm sorry." He pulled her closer and kissed the top of her head, rubbing her back as he held her. "I need to network. You know, after the work I did in L.A., I'm wanting a better paying position."

"I know." She hugged herself a little closer to him. "I just miss you."

He took her face in his hands. "When I get back tonight, I'll make it up to you, okay?"

She found a smile tugging at the corners of her mouth, despite herself. "Yes, Noel."

"That's my girl." He briefly kissed her lips. "I'll be home later. And I promise I'll keep you company then, yes?"

She nodded. "Of course."

He left, and Gloria ate her dinner, alone, at one of the stools in Noel's tiny kitchen. She pulled the curtains open so that she could see the lights of the city down below the flat, cars and shuttles moving along the streets, making her feel a little less alone.

She tried to think about how she'd occupied her time when she'd lived a similar lifestyle to the one she and Noel had—when she'd been with Henry—but that didn't make her feel any better. She ended up finishing her dinner and falling asleep on the sofa, watching episodes of a show she'd seen all the way through, more times than she could count.

Sometime much later, she woke when Noel returned, gently shaking her awake, stroking her hair and back.

She smiled, sitting up. "You're home."

"You're tired," he said. "Come to bed."

She hesitated. "When you say, come to bed...?"

"It's so late, Gloria. Why not skip tonight?"

Her chest started hurting again. "Sure."

But he caught her arm. "What's wrong?"

"I need to connect with you, Noel. I've been alone all day. I've missed you."

He took pity on her, kissing her first, just in a gentle way...but then, she moved into his lap, and—despite the fact he'd said that they were too tired—they found that neither of them could deny the needs they'd buried all day.

He flipped her onto her stomach and took her from behind on the sofa, his weight bearing down on top of her as he quickly fucked her.

Something about the quick messiness of it turned Gloria on, but she wasn't fully satisfied when Noel shot a small amount of his cum inside her, then declared it done.

He helped her up and into their bed, saying that, since they'd fucked on the sofa, the sheets wouldn't need changing in the morning...making a practicality of their lovemaking, in a way that was far too reminiscent to Gloria of the way he'd whipped out his phone to read the news the night before, after they'd made love...instead of holding her and running his fingers through her hair and down her back until she fell asleep, as he usually had done.

Gloria couldn't allow herself to believe she'd made a rash decision, that she'd devoted herself to Noel and her dreams of their future together too soon.

She'd risked too much for him, already. She only needed to communicate with him, to let him know that she needed more attention...more *everything*. Because, really...reading the news after sex was a little too much, even for her.

She refused to admit the possibility that they weren't as compatible as the first two weeks of endless sex between the two of them had led her to believe.

She needed to know that she'd left Los Angeles for London, for *something*.

For the true love and future with Noel that she still held out the hope that she hadn't imagined, and romanticised out of nothing.

5

CHAPTER FIVE

Gloria woke the next morning and of course, Noel was already gone. She stretched, then lied in bed...allowing herself for the first time—since it had happened—to think about the encounter she'd had a few days earlier...one she'd tried her hardest to forget about.

She'd been at the store. Unlike Henry, Noel had encouraged her to go out and explore the city on her own. He'd ridden the bus with her and showed her around so that she wouldn't feel lost, so she'd know what routes to take to get to different places she needed to go.

She'd decided to go out one morning and to get ingredients to make her smoothies, wanting to start her diet and fitness regime as early as possible, so that she didn't have a chance to lose the fitness she'd worked so hard to attain in L.A., with her trainer.

She'd found a gym not far from the flat, so she'd gotten a membership there, and Noel had shown her a route in a park near the flat that she could jog or run, which she'd already started doing, each morning when she woke, first thing before she got started on her writing or anything else she needed to do for that day.

While she'd been in the produce section of the store, she'd had her back to the door, and she felt a sharp sizzle going up her spine, making the fine hairs on the back of her neck stand at attention.

She hadn't felt that electricity in the air since...the last time she'd called England her home. She sucked in a deep breath, telling herself it was nothing, that she was only feeling so sensitive because she was back in the same country, if not the same city.

But then, she'd heard a familiar voice, one that had haunted her nightmares and graced her dreams numerous times in the past two years since she'd heard it last.

She added the kale to her basket, then she'd slowly turned...

Across the small market, she saw him. Just his back, but she'd recognize him anywhere, from any angle. She'd spent months memorizing every line of his body, and his every nuance...

Somehow, Henry had ended up in London, unbeknownst to her...and not only in London, but in her particular little corner of the city, the few city blocks that she occupied.

She shook, nearly dropping her basket. She wanted nothing more than to throw down her basket and to run away, far away, back to the safety of that little flat that she shared with her new lover, never to leave it again.

But another part of her—a part she could not deny—drew her toward him, making her insides shake...turning over tender and long-forgotten pieces of her, places of her soul that only Henry had been able to touch, even after all the time that had passed since she'd seen him last.

She slowly approached him, her stomach clenching and her heart pounding.

Perhaps he'd felt that same charge in the air, because Henry had turned around and faced Gloria...for a moment, they did nothing more than stare at each other.

Finally Henry broke the silence. "Imagine meeting you here, babygirl."

She hadn't been able to find her voice. She had stared at him, opening and closing her mouth a few times before she'd had to close it for good.

There was nothing that she could say to him! Not after all that had happened between the two of them...

"Are you going to speak?"

He sounded so cold. But he'd called her "babygirl," conversationally enough...she wasn't sure how to feel.

"I...what are you doing in London?"

"What are you doing in England?" he countered.

She swallowed. "I'm...I moved back."

"Why?"

"Henry...should we be having this conversation?"

She spoke timidly, but tiredly...she felt as though her fear was coming out in her words in a cruel way.

She didn't mean to be cold toward him.

"I don't see what's wrong about it. You're here, and I have no idea why. Not that it matters. I had to leave. Vic made it impossible for me to stay in Blackpool. She was threatening lawyers...I suppose I've got you to thank for that, Gloria."

"I'm sorry."

"You aren't. You got what you wanted. Perpetually the victim. Do you live nearby, Gloria?"

"I'm not going to tell you that."

He nodded. "You do. Why else would you be at this little market, unless you're local? That's fine and good. At least I know that there's someone who wants their asshole used, not far from me, when the need strikes."

She felt her face get hot, and her mood darkened...and goddamn her if tears didn't come to her eyes.

"I've got a boyfriend, Henry," she said, her voice trembling as she spoke.

"I bet he doesn't use your ass, though. Sure he wouldn't mind sharing."

She turned away from him, deciding that she needed to get out of that store and away from him...the smoothie didn't matter. Maybe she could text Noel and ask him to pick up some kale on his way home from work.

As Gloria lied in her and Noel's bed that morning, though...she couldn't help thinking about how disappointing the sex had been the night before, and Noel's lack of attention. Maybe she was being too hard on him, because he'd just started back at his job...that was a lot of pressure, especially adjusting to his life with her being a part of it.

But then...if he loved her, then it seemed to Gloria as though he would have wanted to come home and spend his evenings with her, especially since she'd sacrificed a lot, in leaving her life in L.A. behind in order to be with him, so that the two of them could be together and could have a future together...

She thought about what Henry had said...the mere fact that Henry was *there*, in fucking London, and close to where she lived.

She had a real possibility of marriage and a family—finally—with Noel; there was no way in hell that she could afford to entertain even the idea of taking Henry up on his offer.

Not that she wanted to, she told herself.

It didn't matter to her if Noel didn't want to fuck her butthole. She'd hated how that was the only thing that Henry had ever seemed to want to do with her, after all.

She had to forget about fucking Henry, once and for all.

She had to forget about *fucking* Henry, too...about how, despite the fact she had hated how he paid far too much attention to fucking her asshole and not nearly enough to her as a human being.

But that was just Henry, and that was how he was. She'd spent a long time coming to terms with that, accepting it and him for what he was, and their relationship for all that it had been.

She got up out of bed and pulled on her pajamas she'd left on the bedroom floor. She'd shucked them, hoping that her naked body curled against Noel's would have ignited some passion in him...he'd just asked if she wasn't cold, and had tossed her another blanket before he'd fallen fast asleep on the opposite side of the bed.

Barely even touching her.

She knew he was sweet and respectful, but sometimes she felt she needed more than that...she needed passion and burning desire, like when they'd first started sleeping together.

She was still unwilling to admit that she'd jumped the gun in moving in with Noel. They would work things out; there was no way that he would go out two nights in a row to leave her alone and lacking.

She went to the kitchen and found his empty coffee mug in the sink. Gloria never left anything sitting around on the kitchen counters or in the sink in her apartment, so she'd taken to cleaning up after Noel. Not that he was messy, but she also didn't want to allow things to get too out of hand, and she didn't have a lot else to do in the mornings. She made herself a smoothie and ate half a muffin to have some carbs to fuel her workout. She went for a run, then came home to shower.

She set up her laptop in the living room of the flat, turning on something mindless for background noise while she got back to where she'd left off on her book the night before. She'd set her timer on her phone for about an hour before Noel was to arrive home, so that she could have plenty of time to get ready...do her makeup, dress nicely, light some candles in the bedroom.

So she was extremely disappointed—and unhappy—when Noel arrived home on time...with a strange woman that Gloria had never seen, or even heard of.

"Gloria, my darling," he said, kissing her hair in greeting, "this is my best mate, Ryn."

Gloria had a hard time even conjuring a tiny smile for her. "Hi."

"I've heard so much about you, Gloria."

"I wish I could say the same."

Noel at least seemed bright enough to pick up on the fact that she was unhappy about his guest, especially taking in Gloria's carefully applied makeup and sensual outfit. "I should have told you, Gloria."

She didn't respond. "Excuse me for a moment."

She went to the bedroom and blew out the candles she'd lit...no need in wasting a $130 candle when they wouldn't be in the bedroom to enjoy it.

She took a few deep breaths, trying to calm herself. She wasn't happy at all that Noel had brought a woman home with him, period...especially without telling her, but she didn't even like the thought of his best friend being a woman.

He'd never given her any indication while they'd been together back in L.A. that he had a close female friend. He'd acted like she was the most important thing in his universe.

Had it all been a ruse? Had she made a massive mistake?"

She started to go back out into the kitchen, but she hesitated in the doorway of the bedroom, hearing Ryn—and what kind of a fucking name was *that?*—and *her* boyfriend having a heated conversation.

"Your girl doesn't want me here."

"That isn't so," Noel said.

"You didn't tell her I was coming?"

"I didn't think she'd mind."

"She clearly had other plans for the two of you tonight."

Gloria frowned, not liking the hint of irritation at the thought of Gloria wanting to sleep with her boyfriend, that Ryn apparently felt.

She decided it was time to step back into the kitchen, to make her presence known. She crossed her arms over her chest as she stood just outside the kitchen.

"Gloria, you don't mind that Ryn is here, do you?"

"Like she's going to answer that question with me standing right here," Ryn protested.

Gloria didn't like the familiarity with which Ryn spoke to Noel. Noel was *hers,* and Ryn had the attitude of a woman who was scolding her lover.

"You're right, Ryn, in that I don't appreciate your presence here."

They both stared at her like she'd said something terrible...then Ryn's face got red.

"Right. I'll just be leaving, then."

"Ryn, don't go," Noel said.

Gloria stared at him...was he *really* choosing his friend over her? Because if he tried to convince his friend not to go, instead of reassuring Gloria that she was the rightful center of his universe...

"Oh, fuck, no," Gloria said, in disbelief.

"Gloria, I don't understand why you're upset."

"Then you're clueless, and it's no wonder you've only dated two girls in your life." She shook her head, infuriated. "Fuck this. You know what, Ryn? I'll leave. You stay here with Noel." She frowned at him. "It's clear to me that he'd rather spend his evenings with anyone other than me."

"Gloria—"

She didn't wait to hear anything else from him. Instead, she went to the bedroom and grabbed a trench coat out of her closet, put on some shoes, grabbed her bag, her laptop, and her phone, and she left Ryn and her boyfriend alone in their flat...to likely continue whatever it was they'd been up to before she came into the picture.

6

CHAPTER SIX

Anger fueled Gloria's trip down to the late-night café right around the corner from the flat, but by the time she had her chai tea and was seated in a secluded corner of the café, her anger had been replaced by the despair she felt over having been—apparently and until proven undoubtedly otherwise—fucked over by another man she trusted and had given her body and soul to.

Blinded by the tears that threatened to spill down her cheeks, biting down hard on her lower lip, she stared at her laptop screen for a few moments before her fingers furiously began pounding out more of her story...that was turning into more of a eulogy to love than the respite and comfort she'd intended it to be.

But as the words she wrote reflected the emotions she felt, more than anything else, she went with it, allowing herself to spill out all of her anger, hurt, frustration, and fear into her keyboard, forming the next story she'd pen, that would suck away just a little bit more of her soul.

She was lost in it, having no idea of the hour or of her surroundings, when she was aware of someone approaching her, pulling out the seat across from her and taking their seat at her table.

She lifted her bleary eyes to see the second-to-last person she wished to see.

Henry.

She swallowed. "Did you follow me here?"

"I would ask the same of you. To be fair, this place has been my refuge since I moved here. I come here late in the evenings to be alone with my thoughts."

She raised her eyebrows. "And I'm supposed to believe that, Henry?"

"Have I ever lied to you?"

"You're really asking me that?"

He held her gaze. "Be honest. Don't allow your apparent anger toward me to cloud your judgment of what we had, Gloria. Did I ever lie to you?"

"You...you had all of those messages on your phone," she whispered.

"Yes. Which you never would have known about, had you not invaded my privacy. Do you have any idea what happened to me when you fled for the U.S., babygirl?"

She felt her brow furrow. "Don't call me that."

"Why ever not? Because you like it a little too much, don't you?"

She shivered, but tried to hide it by shrugging...judging by the look that Henry gave her, though, she hadn't succeeded.

"Be honest."

"You never lied to my face, no. But you snuck around behind my back. And you made me believe that you were a gentleman, when you...god, Henry, what you did to your ex-wife is unforgivable."

Without warning, Henry reached across the table and grabbed Gloria's hand firmly in his, painfully. She tried to pull away...but then, something about his grip, the way he touched her...it took her back to when she'd been his, and she was powerless to resist him.

When she glanced up to meet his eyes, Henry saw that, and he nodded. "Good girl. Now that you remember who you are, maybe we can actually make some progress."

"I'm not your good girl anymore, Henry," she whispered.

He smiled, but his wasn't a smile of amusement. "Are you sure about that, babygirl?"

She frowned. "I'm sure. I told you, I've got a boyfriend."

"Do you?" he asked. "Then where is he? This is the second time you told me that you've got a boyfriend, and the second time that I've seen you out alone."

She swallowed.

"If you were mine, babygirl, I wouldn't let you out at night without me."

"My boyfriend doesn't think I'm his property."

"That upsets you, doesn't it?"

"No. Why would it?"

"Does he know how to fuck you properly?"

Gloria shook her head. "Don't talk to me that way."

"You don't like it anymore? The books you write would indicate otherwise."

"Henry."

"Did you move back here because you found a new man?"

"I moved back to England because my boyfriend lives here, yes, but I also wanted a change. I moved to London, Henry, not knowing that you're here now."

"Do you know why I had to move here?" he asked again. "Listen to me. When you left me, you destroyed me. You ruined my life, and you broke my heart."

"You don't have a heart to break, Henry."

"You promised me that you'd always be there when I needed you. I needed you, and you left."

"You were cheating on me."

"I never cheated on you."

"I saw the messages!"

"And they were only messages, Gloria. I never met up with any of them."

It drove a knife through her heart, though...because that was how her husband had done her, messaging a woman he'd ended up getting pregnant.

She stood. "I'm leaving."

"Stay. Talk to me."

She shook her head. "I'm not spending another second of my time being here with you, when I could be at home with the man who actually cares about me."

"You think that I don't care about you?" he asked, almost coldly.

She couldn't help feeling that she was being cruel to him...ironically, considering after two years, he'd told her he only wanted to fuck her ass again.

But that was just how he was.

"Why aren't you at home with your boyfriend, anyway, if he's so wonderful and caring?"

She felt her face pale as she looked at him.

"He's not as perfect as you've made yourself believe, is he, Gloria?"

"He's nicer to me than you ever were."

"Maybe so, but I never lied or cheated on you."

She grabbed her bag and she walked away from him and out of the café...funny how much easier it got to walk away from him, the more times she did it.

She really shouldn't have walked out on Noel. She should have stayed, told him how deeply upset she was by his actions, and they could have worked it out together. But she'd *told* him about how her husband had cheated, and he should have been more sensitive to her needs. Especially after the night before, when she'd made it clear that she'd been upset that he'd left her alone all night when he'd gone out with his friends, not telling her first.

She let herself back into their flat, thinking that she'd find Noel and Ryn still holding court in the kitchen, the other woman acting like she belonged there...she probably thought that she *did* belong, that she'd been in that flat more than Gloria had.

But the flat was silent, and the lights were out. It was later than Gloria had realized, so she took off her shoes and set her things outside the bedroom door, not wanting to be too noisy, since apparently Noel was asleep.

She planned to undress in the dark and slip into bed beside him, curling up against him. She hoped he'd wake when she got into their bed, and she would apologize, but she would let him know how hurt she'd been.

But the floor lamp was on, illuminating their bedroom with a soft, warm glow...and Noel was in bed, yes.

But so was Ryn.

Gloria stared, feeling horror rise inside her, followed closely by fury.

She surprised herself, though, by quietly letting herself out the bedroom, grabbing her things, putting her shoes back on.

She headed on shaking legs down to the same café again...hoping—although perhaps she shouldn't have—that Henry was still there.

He was in the same seat, facing the window, a cup of coffee between his hands.

Slowly, Gloria found her way back to him, feeling as though she were outside her body watching everything unfold.

Henry felt her presence. He turned to face her, seeing her standing there knowing—intuitively—that something was wrong.

He stood. "Gloria?"

She couldn't hold back any longer, feeling herself shatter. She dropped her handbag and laptop bag at her sides.

Henry stood, and he held open his arms to her. She flung herself at him, clinging to him...finally finding comfort in his embrace again.

She was shocked when she felt tears flowing down her face, and even more shocked when Henry took a napkin and wiped her tears away.

"Don't cry, babygirl," he said, quietly, looking down into her face.

She bit her lip. "Henry..."

"Hey," he said, drawing her close again. "Do you want to get out of here?"

A wiser part of her told her that she needed to step away, that leaving with him was a disaster. That she was hurting and vulnerable, like he was taking advantage of her.

But she nodded.

He paid his tab, and he picked up her bags, placing her handbag over her shoulder, and carrying her laptop bag, himself.

"Come, Gloria."

Her stomach twisted. He'd told her those words before...but when she'd been naked underneath or on top of him. Her face got hot, but she placed her hand in his, as they stepped out of the café, and she looked up to meet his eyes.

"Where do you want to go?" he asked her.

She swallowed. She didn't know...she hadn't thought that far ahead.

"Listen, we can go to my place, but I'm not sure that I can trust you."

She hesitated. "What do you mean?"

"You'll believe any lie you hear about me. Am I to believe that you wouldn't tell any lie about me, either? Am I safe, bringing you into my home?"

Instead of arguing, she knew she needed a place to stay for that night. She couldn't go back to her flat.

"Yes, you can trust me," she whispered, her lips feeling numb as she spoke.

He stared at her a few moments, like he wasn't sure if he could believe her, but he finally nodded. "Fine."

They walked up the opposite end of the block from where Gloria lived. She found herself gripping his hand more tightly, her body pressed against his...as numb as she was, she'd never thought two years ago, when she'd left him, that she would ever feel his touch again...no wonder, then, that she was having a difficult time wrapping her head around it.

"Henry, I only left you because I had to. I didn't want to." She squeezed his fingers. "I was in love. I would have died for you."

He glanced down at her as they walked. "But you wouldn't have stayed for me, and you'd believe any lie my ex-wife told you."

"Was she lying? Look at me. Look in my eyes, Henry, and tell me that you didn't do that to her."

He grabbed her chin, somewhat roughly. "I don't have to invite you into my home. Keep that in mind."

She gasped, then glanced down. "Yes, Henry."

The words had come without her thinking. But as soon as she'd spoken them, she felt his touch soften.

"Good girl," he said, softly...just like no time had passed at all.

Perhaps their love was timeless, or she was simply a fool. Either way, it felt right.

Either way, she was with Henry, again.

Just as he'd said, just like that.

He led her into his building, up to his flat, and he opened the door, pushing it open. "Go on."

It was dark inside. Still, Gloria did as he'd told her, walking right into the flat, despite the fact she could see nothing, and she'd done it because he'd told her to.

He came in behind her, flicking on the light and closing the door. His presence pushed her further inside, and she shivered.

"It's not much. Of course, neither was my house where you lived with me, but I lost even that to my ex wife. Despite the fact she'd taken the house where the children grew up."

She wasn't sure how to respond, so she simply looked at him, wishing she could speak, wishing that she could have managed to do anything at all, other than to simply stare at him.

"Have you nothing to say, babygirl?"

She shook her head. "I'm sorry."

He set down her laptop. "Make yourself comfortable, Gloria. You may as well."

His flat was strikingly similar to Noel's, except that Noel's was decorated and arranged differently. Henry had a green sofa, a smaller flat screen, and a giant coffee maker in his kitchen.

She couldn't even look in the direction of his bedroom.

She sat on his sofa, swallowing, her heart in her throat. She felt afraid, yes, like a cornered animal...but she'd chosen to be there—with Henry—in spite of the consequences.

"Would you like a drink?"

"Better not," Gloria replied, in a tremulous voice.

He came around and sat on the sofa, close to her...but not too close. She looked at him.

"You look at me as though you fear me," he said.

"Perhaps I do."

"If I wanted to hurt you, Gloria, then I would have done so already."

"Why did you invite me back here?"

"Why did you return to the coffee shop, babygirl?"

"I went back home, and there was another girl in his bed."

She couldn't believe she'd told Henry that. Her most shameful truth, and she'd shared it with the one person who could hurt her the most, if he so chose.

"I'm sorry," Henry said.

She almost believed him.

"How long has this been going on?"

"I don't know. I barely know Noel. I've only been dating him for three weeks."

"I suppose you hadn't known me much longer before you moved here with me."

"I'm stupid," she said.

"You're not stupid, Gloria, you just don't like to admit to the truth of how you already know people to be. You knew he wasn't trustworthy, but you moved here with him anyway, thinking you could make him into the man you wanted.

"Just as you did with me."

"Henry...were you truly not lying to me about your ex-wife?"

He stretched. "I find it fascinating that you're wanting the truth now, when you've already ruined my life."

"Henry..."

"She took my little house we shared together. It was the last thing I had left of you, and she took that from me. She took my children from me, she took our home...then she took you away."

"She only helped me to leave you."

"After you promised me that you never would," he said, looking into her eyes from across the sofa. "Do you remember making me that promise, babygirl?"

"You were unfaithful to me."

"That's a matter of opinion, isn't it?"

She shook her head. "That's how my husband cheated on me, too."

"Your husband? Is it, then? Hmm, seems you should have stayed with me then, doesn't it? Your ex-husband cheated, and you found your now boyfriend in bed with another woman, correct? Or am I mistaken?"

"That's correct, Henry," she said.

"Well, babygirl, I guess I wasn't as bad as you thought."

"Henry," she said, softly, a pleading note in her tone, "I'm hurting."

He moved closer to her, wrapping her arm around her shoulder as he drew her body against his, on his sofa. "And don't you ever think about how you left *me* hurting when you left, Gloria?"

"I had to leave. You gave me no other option."

"I saw you and your boyfriend together, Gloria."

"When?" she asked, her voice soft.

"Does it matter?"

"If it doesn't matter, why did you even bring it up?"

"Just that I know my competition, and I felt confident in bringing you home with me again tonight."

"I tried talking to you, Henry, not long after we broke up."

"I remember."

"You made it clear to me that I didn't matter, that you didn't still want me. So how was I supposed to know that you were hurting so badly?"

"You should have known me well enough to be able to tell, babygirl. I'm deeply hurt that you apparently didn't realize the damage you'd done.

"I let my guard down. I fell in love with you, again. I trusted you, again, after my ex-wife, and you betrayed me, just the same."

She swallowed. She was still naive enough to believe his words, to truly think she'd been the one to hurt him, that he wasn't manipulating her, just as he'd done for all the months they'd been together.

"You know me, and I know you. I know I hurt you, babygirl, but you're not the only victim in all of this. And all the men you've been with after me, all the ones who have hurt you...you knew exactly what you were doing."

"I was trying to find someone who could make me feel the way that you did, but someone who wouldn't hurt me. There's only one you, Henry. And I still fucking want you."

Henry stared at her. In that moment, she felt as though she were coming apart in all the ways that mattered, and that—again—he was shaping her into who he wanted her to be.

"I could never deny you anything, babygirl."

Gloria flinched. She *hated* when he called her that, like no time had passed since they'd been together, like he'd not burned that bridge like it was a savage vampire he needed to destroy.

She had spent two years trying her hardest to recover from what he had done to her. Through every action she took, the books she wrote, the men she dated, she had been trying—for *two years*—to move past him.

And there she was. Back in his country, back in his house, about to ruin her life all over again. She knew he hadn't changed; he was exactly the same man who had come into Gloria's life two years earlier and turned it upside down. She'd left Georgia, and her family's protection, to go be with this vile, cruel man across the Atlantic. She'd moved to England to be with him. She'd turned her back on said family, and on their fortune, to which she had been an heiress, before *she* had burned *that* bridge...and she'd done it all for him.

For that fucking man.

"You're a liar, Henry," Gloria said, lifting her head and squaring her shoulders as she stared at him. "You lie to everyone. To all the women you sleep with, to your family...but most of all, you lie to yourself. You truly believe that you're a gentleman, don't you?"

"I've not knocked you flat yet. You still believe yourself to be the victim, I see."

"Henry."

"If you didn't want to be here, you wouldn't have come here. You wanted everything that I did with you back then, and you want it again, now. Why else would you be standing in my living room again, Gloria Alexander?"

He didn't wait for her response to his irresistible monologue. He knew how to work her, how to manipulate her in order to get exactly what he wanted from her.

But Gloria had new tricks up her sleeves. She wasn't the agreeable, naive woman he'd turned inside out two years earlier.

"Your new man," he repeated. "So what, you like brown guys now?"

"I like men who aren't complete selfish assholes."

"Yet, he cheated on you like a selfish asshole. Why did you return to the coffee shop tonight, Gloria?"

"I had nowhere else to go," she whispered.

"Is that the case? Or did you want to run to my arms again, thinking that, despite what you did to me, I'll still take you back and get you addicted to my cock again?"

"I could get cock anywhere I wanted. That's not what I want. You know that. You knew it from the beginning. I need *more*, Henry."

"Marriage and babies."

"You almost gave me that."

He trailed his fingers over her face, slowly allowing his fingers to almost reach down to her neck, but he hesitated, teasing her, she couldn't help thinking.

"Show me how much you need me, babygirl. Show me that you want me to be your man again."

"Why? Nothing I did was ever enough for you in the past."

"I think that you know exactly how to win me over, Gloria. You've always known my weaknesses. My heart on my sleeve."

"I don't think that you have a heart," she whispered, her lower lip trembling in anticipation and fear.

"I do, and you stole it from me."

"Then why were you so cruel to me? Henry, we tried. I tried. I wanted it so badly. You know that I did. And I thought that if I gave you another child..."

"That I would take care of you."

"No," she said, grabbing his hand. "I thought that we could be a family, and that we could take care of each other."

He shook his head. "You're a writer. You have a way with words. It's easy for you to use pretty language and beautiful imagery to convince a man that his heart is safe in your hands. You're paid a lot of money to do so, after all."

"What do you want from me, Henry? Do you want me to tell you that I love you?

"You broke me of that. And, don't worry. The parts of me that weren't broken when you were done with me...the men who came after you took care of those."

He moved his fingers from their soft caresses of her cheeks, to a firm grip around her neck. "No, Gloria. That isn't what I want."

"Then I have no business being here with you."

Gloria made no move to get up off of his sofa and to remove herself from his presence, though. She remained pinned by his touch to his sofa, trembling, tears in her eyes.

"I couldn't see you in pain. I handled things badly. I can't blame you for wanting to leave. Although, I fail to see why you needed to destroy my life in the process."

"You wouldn't believe me," she whispered.

He leaned in, his forehead touching hers, his lips so close that she could taste his breath. "I'll tell you what I want from you, Gloria Alexander. That is your name, still, isn't it?"

"Gloria Wilcocks. I never changed it back after my divorce."

"I don't like that another man gave you his name. Didn't he know that you were already mine?" Henry asked, tracing the tiny, faded tattoo on the inside of her ring finger.

She moaned. She couldn't respond to him.

She'd felt it. Even after she'd left Henry, she was still his. It was why she'd never really moved on. Why she'd fucked Alex, why she'd been desperate to submit to Donovan...why she'd gone around and around in her genuine love affair with Javier, because he'd had the attitude and sex she craved...but Bryson had the stability, and was willing to offer it to her.

Except when he'd decided he wanted something else.

And Noel...she'd moved back to England because she loved it there, yes, but more so because being there, she would feel more connected to herself.

To Henry.

When she'd seen him there in that grocery store, then again in the coffee shop...when life gave Gloria a chance, she'd never turned her back on it in the past.

She could never turn her back on Henry again, despite the fact that she knew he had the power to destroy her, far beyond repair.

She was Henry's. His property, his whore, and his lover, if he wanted her to be.

His wife, if fate would allow...although she was terrified to allow herself to hope for that. She'd felt it from the moment she'd first spoken to him, that Henry was it, for her. She knew she would have spent the rest of her life looking for what she'd found in him, in any other man...

She was submitted already. If he only wanted a whore to visit when the mood struck him, then Gloria would spread her ass cheeks for him and take him inside her.

If he wanted a wife to torture, she'd bear that burden, as long as she got to love him, in exchange for her agony.

Henry drew her into his arms, much like he had done in the coffee shop, a comforting and safe embrace that made her feel whole again, for the first time since she'd last slept beside him. It wasn't the same kind of safety she'd felt with Bryson. Her heart wasn't safe with Henry.

But she knew that he was worth the pain of loving him.

He kissed her neck, making her shiver, then he whispered into her ear, "I want you to make love to me, Gloria. Be a good girl and make love to me, like we used to."

Stubbornly, she still resisted. "I'm not who I used to be. I've changed, a lot."

"No kidding? Show me. I want to see you now. Naked. I want to feel you," he said, drawing her into his lap.

"No," she resisted, putting her hands against his chest, pushing him back.

"Come now, babygirl. I know you've been dreaming about this." He brushed her hair back from her shoulders.

Gloria flinched away from his touch, shivering as his fingertips grazed her collarbone ...she clenched her jaw, putting distance between them.

"Are you afraid, babygirl?"

"No," she said.

She *was* afraid, though. She was terrified. She longed for his touch again, needing to know how accurate the version of his touch that existed in her memories was.

His touch, his kiss...god, she longed to feel his lips on hers again.

But he was awful. He wanted her again because he was bored, because she was—or so he thought, as she had been once—an easy target.

"Stop, Henry!"

He sighed, frustrated...he was so close that she could smell his sweet scent, could taste his breath, which did nothing to ease her frustration and fear.

He moved slightly away.

She swallowed. "I can't take this. I can't be alone with you. I can't cheat on Noel."

"Why not? He's cheating on you."

She frowned at him.

"That's the problem with dating London guys, Gloria. There's too much temptation in a city so large. Too many women."

"How many women were you cheating on me with, Henry?" she asked.

"I wasn't."

"I saw your fucking phone, Henry. I read the messages. All those women in your dms?"

"That really got to you, didn't it?"

"Yes. You betrayed me in a lot of ways."

"You hurt me too, you know," he said, his eyes darkening.

She flinched, remembering his violence, how she'd been so afraid of him, in his apartment back in Blackpool.

"Why are you suddenly afraid?" he asked.

"Because you could hurt me."

"Don't you believe, Gloria, that if I wanted to hurt you—truly—that I would have done so by now?"

She shrugged. "Maybe you're waiting for the perfect opportunity."

"Or, maybe I don't wish to do you any harm."

"You don't care about me," she said, flatly.

"If I didn't care about you, why would I have taken you in my arms and given you a place to sleep tonight?"

"Stop." Her blood ran cold.

"Stop, what?" he asked, curiously.

"You know exactly what you're doing. You're talking down to me."

"And why would I do that, Gloria?" he asked.

He'd been slowly moving closer again. She'd barely noticed, having been so caught up in their conversation, in protecting herself.

But he was so close, then, that there was no denying it..

"Because you know what it does to me. And because you want to take advantage of me."

He laughed. "I wouldn't have to try."

"Henry," she said, warning in her voice.

"I could have you on your knees and being ass-fucked by me in a heartbeat, babygirl, and you know it."

"No," she said. "Stop. Give me space, Henry."

"This is my house, Gloria. You know that you're free to go at any time."

She clenched her jaw. But, then she surprised herself by asking, "How did I hurt you, Henry?"

"You left me."

"You pushed me away. You *forced* me away," she said.

"You were unkind to me, as well."

"What the fuck did I do?" Gloria demanded.

"You asked me for too much."

"Then why did you keep giving it to me? Why ask me to marry you? Why invite me to move to England so that I could be with you, if you didn't want it all?"

"Because you wanted it, Gloria!"

She stared at him.

Henry sighed. "You wanted it, and I can't deny you anything, babygirl."

It was the second time he'd said it since she'd come into his home.

That had to mean something...but perhaps merely the fact that Gloria insisted on believing that to be true said more about her than she wished it would.

"You talked to other women, you were cruel to me, and you threatened me."

"You know what I'm like. Why did you leave, instead of trying to work it out with me?"

"You made me feel like you didn't want to work it out. You told me you wouldn't change, and I told you that I wouldn't try to change you."

He eased closer to her. "I loved you. Gloria...if you would have kept pushing me..."

"You hated it when I pushed you," she whispered.

He reached out and cupped her cheek in his hand...his touch was glorious, and Gloria relaxed beneath it.

"I want you, Gloria. Please. You're here, you have no reason to remain faithful to a man who isn't faithful to you. Do you want this?"

She opened her eyes, chewing her lip, hard. "Yes."

He leaned in. "Show me, babygirl."

She reached her hand behind his head and cupped his neck, pulling him closer to her, pressing her lips against his. God, the taste of him...her memories hadn't done his kiss justice. He was delectable, wonderful...his touch was equal parts comfortable familiarity and terrifying urgency. She knew what kind of a man he was. She knew his tastes and preferences...she knew what it was like to be in his bed every night.

And, again, there she was.

Her lips moved slowly against his. He was patient and gentle as she remembered him, as she recognized and became reacquainted, as she craved, harder and harder.

She moaned softly, and he made a motion with his hands on her hips...it was all the encouragement that Gloria needed. She climbed right back into his lap and wrapped herself around him, feeling his hard bulge against her leg.

"Henry," she moaned, running her fingers through his hair.

He eased his hands up her dress, pushing it up to her waist. She felt no shyness or shame...too turned on to think about any of those things.

She wrapped her legs around his waist as she kept kissing him, using her tongue to caress his lips. He opened his, and she eased her tongue into his mouth. He grabbed the back of her neck and held her there, thrusting his tongue against hers.

She clenched her thighs together. Since her legs were wound around Henry's waist, though, it wasn't easy to do. Henry picked up on her desires, though, and he put one arm around her waist and stood, carrying her with him as he took her right to his bedroom.

No matter how dangerous and wrong it was, Gloria didn't care at all, in that moment...all that mattered to her was that she was getting ready to finally fuck him again, when she'd dreamed of it—he'd been right about that—for two years.

He shoved the bedroom door open with his foot, and it hit the wall with the force of his kick as he carried her to the bed at the center of the room, lying her down across it.

Her heart was pounding so loudly that she could barely hear...she was panting, shaking.

Henry stood over her. He could tell the effect he had on her, easily.

"I've missed you," he told her.

"I missed you for so long. I'm not sure I ever stopped missing you."

"You know that I was in love with you, right?"

She bit her lip.

He frowned. "You didn't know it."

"Henry..."

"Don't worry about it, babygirl. Remember what I said? I want you to make love to me. Will you do that, Gloria?"

"Yes," she whispered, helplessly.

He stood over her, still, as he unbuttoned his shirt. She whimpered as she watched him undressing.

Then she couldn't bear him taking off his clothes as she watched. "Henry, please. Get in bed with me."

He smiled, and it was the most genuine smile she'd seen from him in ages...so long she couldn't even remember.

He climbed onto the bed, over her, his knees and elbows on either side of her. He moved so quickly over her that her head was spinning...but she quickly recovered, reaching up to push his shirt off of his shoulders.

She fingered his tattoo on his arm, then she ran her hand over his chest. She hadn't thought she'd ever get to touch him again, and there he was, in front of her, beneath her touch.

She'd waited two years.

She was ready to indulge in him.

7

CHAPTER SEVEN

Gloria's breathing was still erratic as she ran her hands over Henry's arms and chest, sighing softly as she felt the familiar lines of his body. She glanced up to meet his eyes, and she wished she hadn't...the way that he was looking at her terrified her.

His gaze wasn't dark or dangerous. That would have been far more comforting...but instead, his gaze was almost worshipful. He'd never worshipped her! He'd used her, and that had been what got her addicted to him in the first place.

He held himself over her, watching her as she explored his body...but he still hadn't touched her. He wasn't even looking at her body; he was watching her face.

It made her insides shake. It stupidly made her think that—maybe—he actually loved her, and that he cared about her as a human, not as merely a fuck puppet, as she'd always believed.

"I missed you."

He lowered himself beside her on his bed, cupping her cheek in his hand as he looked into her eyes. "I missed you, babygirl. You have no idea how much."

She wanted to believe him, of course. How couldn't she have? But she still held onto that tiny piece of her sanity that still thought clearly enough to tell her that she needed to be careful.

That he wasn't in love. He never had been.

That what she knew to be true was their reality: that Henry didn't have the capacity to love. He could fuck, and he could fuck *well*, but he didn't love her.

"Stop holding back, Gloria."

"How do you know...?"

"I know you," he said, pulling her closer, kissing her head. "I know you better than you know yourself. Isn't that what you always told me?"

"Yes, Henry."

"Take my pants off of me."

She sat up, reaching down to unbuckle his belt. She nervously glanced up to meet his eyes...wondering if he intended to use his belt on her later on. She'd never liked being hit with the belt. It was painful, it was cruel, it didn't turn her on. She'd always felt like Henry had been punishing her for something she hadn't done...and she began wondering, for the first time in the course of their relationship, who Henry *had* been punishing, when he'd beaten her.

He reached out to stroke her arm. "Don't worry, Gloria. I won't hurt you."

She whimpered, then quickly undid his fly and eased his trousers down. He lifted his hips, allowing her to undress him. She tossed his pants aside and traced the outline of his cock through his underwear.

He moaned at her touch, and she smiled, meeting his eyes.

"No one can make me feel the way that you make me feel, babygirl."

She took a deep breath. "It's because no one loves you like I love you."

He held her gaze for a long moment. Gloria felt her heart soaring in her chest...she was so stupid. She knew better. He knew how to manipulate her.

But she did not care.

She moved between his legs and tugged his underwear down, his dick springing free, hard and ready for her.

Slowly, she reached out and took him in her hand...she'd memorized how he felt, his shape, his size, his hardness. She'd felt him inside every hole, so many times. All the other men she'd slept with couldn't erase Henry's impact on her.

She rubbed up and down his length, taking his head between her fingers, making him moan, a deep, guttural noise that spoke to her on a primordial level.

Then she took his tip between her lips, sucking him, already tasting his precum. Henry had traditionally been so reserved and in control of himself...the idea that, having only had him with her for maybe half an hour, she had him so close to losing that carefully maintained control already, turned her on.

She wanted his cock inside her. She wanted to feel that blunt head stretching her, forcing her open. Yes, it was painful, but loving Henry was painful. It made sense. It seemed right.

She took him deeper into her mouth. She kept expecting him to force his way in, to grab her hair and start roughly fucking her face, but he didn't. She finessed him, licking, sucking, looking up into his eyes as she ran her hands up and down his shaft, taking him in a little deeper, letting his head touch the back of her throat.

Henry didn't allow it to go on much longer, though. But instead of grabbing her hair or her neck, he placed his fingers against the side of her face, gently pulling her face off his cock, so she would look into his eyes.

She wasn't sure how to decipher his expression. She swallowed. "Henry?"

"I only want your lips on mine tonight, babygirl."

She flinched. "Was I not...you didn't like it?"

Gloria hadn't lacked confidence in her oral sex skills in years, but within seconds, Henry had done it to her.

"Don't be stupid, Gloria. I spent two years dreaming of having your lips wrapped around my cock. It's just that I've missed your touch and your company more than I missed how your body feels underneath mine. Come here and kiss me."

It wasn't that he was suddenly the perfect gentleman, her ideal lover. He was still bossy and rude, and she knew in her gut that his kindness and tenderness was a ruse to get her to let her guard down so that she'd be stupid and let him in again, so that he could desroy her anew, to make her pay for leaving him before.

He patted the area of his mattress beside him, motioning for her to occupy that space. And wasn't it where she had wanted to be for the past two years? Wasn't it Henry she'd been trying to find, or to forget, in all of the men she'd slept with, even in the man she'd married?

Hadn't she convinced herself, secretly, in those sleepless nights spent in bed alone, crying so hard she thought she'd die after Bryson had divorced her, that the reason she'd suffered so much was because she'd left Henry, the man she'd been made for...that her whole purpose in life was to love that man, or to die trying?

She was terrified.

"Don't look at me like that," he said.

"I wasn't—"

"As though you're afraid."

"I *am* afraid, Henry," she whispered, even with her hand still wrapped around his erect cock.

"Why?"

"You're the only man who can destroy me, Henry. Not even my husband divorcing me did that. But just thinking about how things ended between us...and how they were when we were together.

"That is what hurt the most, my love," she whispered.

He took a deep breath. "It's been so long since you've said that to me. 'My love.'"

She chewed her lip, uncertain of how to respond, and afraid of saying the wrong thing at the same time.

"Did you mean it?"

"Henry."

"Please. At least come here and kiss me."

She shook her head. "I can't do this."

He grabbed her wrist. "Can't do what? Kiss me? You didn't' seem to have any trouble sucking my cock."

"I can't...I can't live through being hurt by you again."

He tugged her sharply up the bed, toward him. She flinched in pain, but he enveloped her in his arms just as quickly.

"Do you want to leave? Maybe we're both better off alone."

"No," she said. "Please don't hurt me again. Please don't fuck with me."

"I told you I wanted you to make love to me. I've dreamed about this happening for two years. You have no idea what it was like after you left me."

"You're manipulating me," she said.

"No, Gloria, I'm not!"

She flinched at his raised voice. He sighed, giving her hand a squeeze. "I'm sorry. I didn't mean to upset you."

"Henry, I want to believe you more than anything. But you hurt me in the past, and I'm not normally stupid enough to fall for the same shit twice."

"I mean it. I want you. I want to love you and I want to give you everything."

"Everything?" she asked.

Foolishly daring to hope...

"Yes, babygirl. Everything."

She didn't care how much it was going to hurt. In that moment, there was nothing she wanted more than what he was promising her...love, gentle sex, and a future.

With him.

She whimpered, placing her hand against his face. "Henry."

He wrapped his arms around her waist and drew her against him. He looked into her eyes, and she believed him...she believed his pain in losing her, how he regretted it, and how he wanted her again.

Forever.

Slowly, she leaned in, closing her eyes, sucking in a breath before she pressed her lips against his.

The shock of feeling his mouth underneath hers made her shiver, bringing tears to her closed eyelids. God, how could she still love him, and so completely? She was mad for him. She always had been, no matter what she'd tried to convince herself of.

He kept his lips soft as she curved hers against his, remembering what he liked, how much pressure. At first, she only kissed his lips, then she felt his tongue gently against her lips, easing his way inside. She parted her lips and allowed him to ease his tongue inside her mouth...gently. He carefully molded his mouth against hers, caressed her tongue with his own.

She clung to him, all of her walls coming down immediately. All it had taken—as always—was a few sweet words and a gentle kiss. She would give him all of her—again—and she would open herself up to being destroyed by him.

Again.

She had to pull away from him, choking on a sob.

He took her by her shoulders. "Gloria, what's the matter?"

She shook her head. "I love you."

He took her face in his hands. "Gloria. It's okay."

She held his gaze, tears streaming down her face. "No, it isn't okay. Because once we have a few good weeks, you're going to get tired of me. Just like you did before."

"No," he said. "I never got tired of you. That's what you're not hearing about this, babygirl. I never wanted to push you away."

"Do you think abusing and intimidating me made me want to stay with you?"

"Babygirl, it's the only way I know how to treat women."

She swallowed.

He held her hands. "Please stop crying, I hate to see you in pain."

She instinctively took him in her arms. "I deserve it for what I did to you. I wanted retribution, Henry, but the only person I ended up hurting was me. I couldn't just walk away from you, either."

"It's okay. You're here with me, now."

She buried her face in his hair. "You don't know how badly I want to believe you."

He wrapped his arms around her waist. "Believe me. Babygirl, I'm all yours. I have been since the day you left."

She stroked his bare back. "What do you mean?"

"I know you've had lovers, and you were even married...and you have no idea how badly it hurt me to know you'd married another man, that he got the life that I wanted with you, and that you were warming some other fucker's bed when you never should have left mine."

She lifted his face to hers. "I'm all yours. I said your name during sex with my ex-boyfriend."

"Of course you did, babygirl."

He seemed pleased by that, so she kissed him again, gratified by him flipping her over, underneath him, carefully positioning his body over hers.

He reached down to ease her dress off over her head, leaving her naked soon after. His gaze feasted on her body for a few moments, then he was back over her, kissing her, stroking her face and pushing her hair back. She wrapped her legs around his waist and her arms around his back, rubbing and stroking him, then gently scratching his back with her fingernails.

He moaned, moving his mouth to her neck.

It all happened quickly after that, but delectably, as Henry eased between her thighs, stroking down between the lips of her labia, her clit, and slipping two fingers inside her as he continued moving his mouth from her neck to her lips, and back again.

She was whimpering, then softly pleading for him. He smiled, removing his fingers from inside her, then pressing them against her lips, so that she could take them into her mouth.

"Good girl," he said, making her even wetter.

He reached down once more, as though he were making sure that she was wet enough, then to position himself to thrust inside her.

His lips were on hers when he entered her. She gasped and flinched.

He noticed, feeling the brief tension in her body at his—albeit welcome—intrusion.

"Surely that didn't hurt, babygirl."

"I'm just not used to you," she said, smiling softly.

"You never could be."

He pressed deeper inside her, and she opened her thighs wider, welcoming him. She moaned at the stretch, arching her back, clinging to him.

She expected hard thrusts, that he'd soon flip her onto her stomach and start forcing himself into her butt, but he kept thrusting, slowly and deliberately. He twisted his hips intermittently, positioning himself and her body so that he hit all the most delicious areas inside her.

He moved his mouth to her neck, licking, kissing, sucking, and biting, his hands on her breasts, cupping her, gently playing with her nipples.

Everything was soft and gentle, and none of it hurt.

She felt herself getting close after only a few thrusts. She angled her hips properly, pushing up against him like she knew he loved.

He never lost it. He was completely aware of what he was doing, but as she rubbed his back and stroked his hair, she felt him gather himself, like he was desperate to cum inside her.

That sent her over the edge. Her back started tingling, and she couldn't feel her toes anymore.

He sank his teeth into her shoulder, and she whimpered. "Please, Henry."

"What, babygirl?"

"I...may I..."

"Yes, Gloria. You don't have to ask my permission," he said, kissing her lips again, before moving his mouth back to her neck. "Not anymore."

She moaned, and he put his mouth back on hers as he came inside her...as they came together.

He held her firmly beneath him, her hips painfully tight against his, as he made her take it all, ride it out with him deep inside her. He buried his face against her breasts, licking her nipples as he kept twitching inside her, and as she clenched around him.

"Oh," she moaned. "Fuck. Henry, I love you."

He ran his mouth back up her neck, finding her mouth with his, kissing her long and hard, before pulling back, cradling her face in his hands. "I love you, Gloria."

She swallowed.

"I really do," he said.

"How do you expect me to just believe you?" she asked, curling against his chest, gripping his bicep in her hand, using her other hand to stroke his chest, feeling his fine, soft hair beneath her hot hand.

He reached up and placed his hand over hers, holding it against him, pressing her palm to him like he was never going to allow her to remove it.

"I wanted to marry you."

"You hated me, Henry. I had to teach myself not to take it personally...that you hate all women."

"I do not hate you, Gloria, I am in love with you. I'm trying to confess my feelings to you. You don't know how difficult this is for me, and here you are, making it more difficult."

"If you loved me, you never would have hurt me. You wouldn't have lied to me, you wouldn't have already been trying to replace me, even while we were still engaged. I was still in mourning when I left you, you know."

His hand found her hair, stroking her, running her fingers through it. "Babygirl, can't you see that I don't know how to process emotions?"

"I'm not your therapist."

"I don't want you as my therapist, babygirl, I want you as my wife."

She shook her head, looking up at him. "I think you're crazy."

"I am. But I want you. I can't go on without you."

She sat up. "Is it truly a coincidence that you ended up in London, and in the same neighborhood as me?"

He nodded. "You don't have to believe me, though. And you don't have to believe that I've mourned you every night since you left me, either. What is faith, if it can be proven?"

"I need you to show me that you love me."

He stared at her a few more moments, then he scooped her in his arms, cradling her neck as he bent his head to hers, kissing her.

She could have allowed him to hold and kiss her like that forever. She would have *loved* nothing more than that.

But she knew his idea of showing he loved her was as twisted as his mind was, and she'd been on the receiving end of that "love" more times than she could recall.

He positioned his body over hers, like he was going to make love to her again...then he tenderly caressed her breasts as he kissed her.

Then he flipped her onto her stomach, yanking down the sheets they had tangled around themselves, revealing her nude backside to him.

She felt his hands cupping her butt, and she moaned softly.

His fingers moved steadily over her buttcheeks. "This is new."

Right. Her tattoo.

"I told you that I wanted this tattoo. I wanted to get it when we got our tattoos together, but..."

"Who took you to get this tattoo, babygirl?"

"My husband," she whispered, into her pillow.

He gave her ass a hard smack, making her gasp, bringing tears to her eyes.

"Do you still like it rough, babygirl?" he asked, easing a finger inside her.

She whimpered.

He slid in another finger, rubbing her, right at her g-spot.

She gasped, lifting her hips, pushing against him so that he went deeper. "I love you."

He positioned himself behind her. "I know it. I love you, Gloria."

"Kiss me," she whispered.

He reached forward, and she turned her head, looking over her shoulder at him. He held her gaze a few moments, then he eased his mouth down over hers.

As he kissed her, he grabbed her hips, squeezing hard, making her whimper in pain.

"Your body has changed."

She felt his fingers exploring her slender, muscular thighs, butt, calves, up to her back. He smacked her ass again, then swiftly moved between her legs, tasting her...but only a lick, a quick dip to sample her.

She gasped. "Henry..."

"You like this, babygirl?" he asked, moving back up her body. He straddled her, holding her shoulders.

"I love it. I love *you*."

"Let me show you how much I love you, Gloria."

He moved back down her body, rubbing her back, kissing her back, her shoulder blades, wetting his fingers inside her before easing them into her butthole.

She flinched. "No."

He flipped her over. "No?'

"You hurt me when you do this. When you put it in my butt. It's painful. I don't enjoy it. At all."

"You don't?"

He seemed genuinely concerned, confused. He cupped her face in his hand. "Why didn't you tell me?"

She bit her lip, hard. "I wanted to keep you happy."

He sighed, pressing his forehead against hers. "Gloria. How many times did I tell you that none of this is enjoyable for me, if you're not enjoying it?"

"What could possibly be comfortable about the man I love fucking my ass and never once making love to me, no matter how good I was?" she asked, gasping.

"Gloria...you always flipped over for me to take your ass. Was I supposed to believe that you hated every minute of it?"

"I wouldn't have minded if you would have been kind to me. I can take anything you want to give to me, physically, as long as you make me feel loved and safe." She sucked in a breath. "And like if I don't *want* to do something, you'll replace me with someone who will."

He reached up to wipe away a tear. "Please. Tell me what you need, Gloria."

She wrapped her legs around his waist, her arms around his shoulders, drawing him close. She held his neck and he pressed his face against her shoulder. She could feel his hot breath on her bare skin, his heart hammering against hers.

"I need you. Only you, Henry. You're all I've ever needed."

"What do you need from me?"

"Forever," she said, stroking the back of his neck, kissing his hair.

She felt him tense, and she tightened her thighs around him. "Relax."

It was so funny her being the one telling *him* to relax, like she posed any threat to him...only, apparently, she did.

His heart.

"If you're faithful and affectionate and loving to me, Henry, if you make space for me in your life and treat me as your equal, then you can have anything you want from me. Why is that so hard for you to believe?"

"My wife made those promises, and she took my children from me."

She could feel him tensing again, so she began stroking his back, opening her thighs subtly so that he was pressed against her...if that didn't ease his tension, she wasn't sure what she could do to him that would.

"I don't have any children to take from you," she whispered.

He sat up, looking at her. "But we will?"

She swallowed. "I hope so."

He ran his hands down her body, making her moan. "I liked your body before, when you had some fat on your hips and thighs."

"Rich men like skinny women, Henry."

He gave her a questioning look.

"My ex was rich."

"I hate him, then, for changing you."

"It's fine, Henry. I hate him for breaking my heart and ruining my life."

"With me, you don't have to push yourself so hard to be physically perfect. I already think you're beautiful."

"You'll make me push myself to please you in bed, though. If you get bored..."

"I've been alone the past two years, alone every night, thinking about you. Obsessing over you, Gloria. Your smell, your warmth, how it felt to sleep with your body pressed against mine...and I've been fucking haunted by the memories of fucking you. I tried to date other women, but none of them were *you*."

"Henry..."

"I can deal with boredom, now that I know what loneliness feels like. I can't live without you, babygirl."

"If you're lying to me...if you break my heart again..."

"Never. I'll marry you tonight if that's what it takes."

She shook her head.

"You don't believe me?"

"How can I believe you, Henry, when you've lied so much? If I didn't want this—desperately—then I wouldn't be here.

"I'm in love," she said, stroking his hair. "I've been in love for two years, no matter what I tried to convince myself of. But if I give you another chance and you break my heart again...I won't get past that."

He took her face in between his hands. "I look at you and I see how broken you are, babygirl. I want to destroy everyone who has hurt you...but I want to destroy them more for touching you than I do for anything else.

"You're mine, Gloria."

She nodded. "I know. I am yours."

He kissed her...and she felt everything in her body rewire in that moment, with the words he'd said and the way he touched her. He wanted her...he still wanted to *own* her, and wasn't that what she'd been wanting so desperately since she'd left him, someone to take ownership and possession of her?

"Henry...are you mine?"

He looked up into her eyes. "In two years, no matter how I tried, I could never love another woman. I think I've been yours since the night you called me 'my love.'"

She smiled softly at him. "That was the first night we spoke."

He cradled her in his arms. "I know."

He kissed her again, more softly that time...she felt a sinking weight in her belly, freezing up, when she should have been losing herself in her lover.

He was so attuned to her, he pulled back, looking at her. "What's wrong, babygirl?"

"How am I supposed to believe that it's going to work, this time? After what you did to your wife..."

"Gloria. You don't understand the whole story."

She hated to admit to herself that she wasn't sure anymore...at that point, anyway, that it mattered to her, either way.

"Will you be with me? Give me a chance. I got a second shot with you, babygirl. I'm not stupid enough to throw that away."

She let out a deep breath. "Okay."

He entered her again, and they made love. He gave her what she needed, which made her want to repay that favor...no longer, though, she knew, because she wanted to please him for fear of losing him, but due to the fact that she loved him so deeply and thoroughly, he made her feel so good that she wanted to give him what he needed because she felt that he'd earned it.

Her trust, her love...

Her complete submission.

Some time later, Gloria couldn't have said how *much* later, though, she was lying underneath him, on her back, with her legs wrapped around him. Never in her life had she felt so at home...not in her mansion on an estate in Georgia, not in her upscale Los Angeles apartment, than she felt there in that little bed, in that tiny flat in London.

It was because she was there with him. With Henry, the only man who had ever really made her love him.

She reached up to touch his face. "Henry, I love you. I'm *in* love with you."

He placed his hand on her face, too, his thumb against her lower lip, which was swollen from all of their kisses.

"You're not allowed to leave me again," she said.

"You're the one who left *me*, Gloria."

She slightly parted her lips, and he eased his thumb into her mouth. She sucked his thumb, making him hard again, making her moan.

She forced herself to breathe. "I'm sorry I believed that you would have done something so cruel."

"I gave you plenty of reason to believe it." He pulled his finger out of her mouth. "I did all of those horrible things to you."

"I liked some of them."

"God, I love you," he replied.

Then he leaned in, over her, kissing her sore lips, ravishing her sore, tender body, making her whole as they both let their guards down, loving each other openly, without the fear of being hurt.

Much later, before they fell asleep due to sheer exhaustion, as the sun was rising and streaming pale light through his windows, she took his shoulders in her hands, looking down at him, as she lied across his chest.

"Henry, let me teach you how to love a woman. Like you taught me how to be a submissive."

He put his hand around the back of her neck. "I would be honored, babygirl."

—•—

EPILOGUE

Two years later

Gloria lied in bed that morning, in no hurry to get a rush start on her day.

She'd just finished her final erotica novel, deciding that she was going to hang up the reins on that particular genre, no longer feeling the need to try to heal herself through the words she wrote. Of course, she still *did* write, as it was her flourishing career...but she had other things in her life at that moment commanding more of her attention.

Ending her relationship with Noel had been easy. He'd not put up a fight, not seemed upset at all when Henry had come to help her take her things out of his apartment that next day, after she'd reunited with her one true love.

Turned out that Noel hadn't realized he was in love with Ryn until that night. Funny thing, that, and Gloria hadn't believed it for a moment, but she also frankly didn't give a fuck. She had enjoyed his uncircumcised cock while it had lasted, but once she had Henry again...no other man existed to her, in her world.

Also, as it turned out, the night that Gloria had spent with Henry after two years had resulted in her conceiving their first child—which was terrifying and overjoying to her at the same time.

Soon after their first daughter was born, Henry and his ex-wife went to mediation, resulting in him being allowed to see his children again. Since he had his new life in London with Gloria and their baby, his children came to London to see him, but she and Henry planned on making a trip to Blackpool sometime when the baby was bigger and ready to travel.

Gloria had never known pain like childbirth, and the weeks that followed, as she healed. Having her baby made it easier to take, but at the same time, she had been so exhausted that it also made her healing more of a challenge.

She discovered how well Henry did with children, though, as he was an equal partner in taking care of their new baby.

Gloria had also never known joy like she'd experienced when she had her baby, and seeing how Henry was with their daughter filled her with hope for their future together...all of them. As much as she ached, already thinking about her baby growing up, she couldn't wait to see what kind of a person her baby would become, when she grew into an adult.

The exhaustion grew more comfortable to Gloria, and she finally healed, and her heart had been filled by how gentle Henry was with her, the first time they had sex after the baby.

He was so good that it hadn't taken them long for her to be pregnant again...that time, with twins, which scared Gloria even *more*, but she also felt like she could handle it, having Henry there to help her.

Things between the two of them weren't perfect. They still had times when Henry got bored, when Gloria got needy, but they worked it out. Perhaps the mediation that he'd done with his ex-wife had helped him in his relationship with her, as well...Gloria didn't care about the reasons behind it; she was just overjoyed by her life.

What had once been a dream she'd soothed herself to sleep with, alone in her giant bed in her L.A. apartment, was now the life that she lived every day, as imperfect and exhausting and sometimes painful as it was.

As rough as Henry could be with her body, he had become so much more tender with her heart, and that was truly all she'd ever needed from him.

Her dreams had become her reality, and she fell asleep in her small bed in their small flat every night, their daughter in her bedroom next door, the crib in the corner of their bedroom for when the twins were born, and Henry. She had Henry every night, his arms around her, sometimes his body inside hers...but either way, and no matter what, she wasn't alone.

She and Henry weren't perfect, but they loved each other deeply, ravenously, and they were both happier than they had ever been, with each other.

THE END.

ACKNOWLEDGEMENTS

I want to thank my readers for loving my stories and for loving Gloria. If she's got a special place in your heart like she does in mine, this book was written for you.

Thank you to my amazing proofreader, Roxana Coumans, for the hard work out into this book, and for my cover designer, Quirky Circe Book Design, for making this book look amazing!

Thank you to my family for supporting my writing career and for always being here, even if there are some books you all aren't "supposed" to read.

ABOUT THE AUTHOR

Teffeteller Myart has been writing her whole life. She graduated from the University of Tennessee, Knoxville, with a degree in English. writing is her primary love, and she plans to continue bringing new stories to her readers for many years to come.

ALSO BY

The Winter Suites Series
Lipstick and Heartbreak, Vol. 1
What Happened in Reno, Vol. 2
The Dirt Bike Rivals (erotic romance novellas)
Jenny's Story
Maggie's Story
Misty's Story
Catharsis (duet)
Absolution (Book One)
Duplicitous (Book Two)

Milton Keynes UK
Ingram Content Group UK Ltd.
UKHW011228280324
440101UK00007B/671

9 798224 750986